*A Candlelight
Ecstasy Romance®*

"YOU CAN'T SLEEP HERE. THAT'S *MY* ROOM!"

"Ah—so you've been sleeping in my bed!" He spread his arms, held on to the doorframe, and leaned in toward her. "Had any interesting dreams? Felt my vibes?"

"I don't want to feel your vibes! And I'm a very sound sleeper—I rarely dream."

"Too bad."

"Suits me fine. And I have another idea." She placed one palm against the front of his shirt and pushed him out of the way. "Why don't you get a room down at Steven's Motel? My treat?" He shook his head, his sky blue eyes never leaving her face. "Then . . . how about friends . . . or somewhere . . ." she whispered, clinging to her last hope.

"I am somewhere . . ." He moved toward her, smiling that irresistible smile. Kate felt suddenly conscious of her own nakedness under the thin shift. "And let's be friends. . . ."

CANDLELIGHT ECSTASY ROMANCES®:

BLUE RIDGE AUTUMN

Natalie Stone

A CANDLELIGHT ECSTASY ROMANCE®

To Our Readers:

We have been delighted with your enthusiastic response to Candlelight Ecstasy Romances®, and we thank you for the interest you have shown in this exciting series.

In the upcoming months, we will continue to present the distinctive sensuous love stories you have come to expect only from Ecstasy. We look forward to bringing you many more books from your favorite authors and also the very finest work from new authors of contemporary romantic fiction.

As always, we are striving to present the unique, absorbing love stories that you enjoy most—books that are more than ordinary romance.

Your suggestions and comments are always welcome. Please write to us at the address below.

Sincerely,

The Editors
Candlelight Romances
1 Dag Hammarskjold Plaza
New York, New York 10017

CHAPTER ONE

Kate Harrington was up to her elbows in pig. The pink bristles scratched against the bare skin of her forearms, and she tugged once again at the inert, uncooperative form, all one hundred and fifty pounds of bottle-fed ham, lying on the surgery table before her.

"Times like this," she muttered, slapping her palm affectionately against the pig's recumbent flank, "I think I should have stayed in Philadelphia and taken care of pussycats and poodles. Move over, Molly!"

The pig, totally anesthetized by the injection Kate had given moments before, did not budge. Again Kate tugged at its short forelegs and succeeded in rolling the pig onto its back. There, inside the right front leg, was the problem. "Silly pig—" Kate murmured, her dark eyes flashing with concern. "Who told you to get into that bailing wire, anyway. You should have stayed with all your buddies and kept out of trouble." She tapped a tapered forefinger gently on the upturned snout, remembering that frosty January morning nine months ago when she had helped deliver this same piglet. It had been during her first weeks on rounds with the Hickory Ridge Animal Clinic when it was bitter cold, the wind whistling and whining down off the heavily wooded slopes of the Blue Ridge Mountains. Doctor Will Turner had been waiting for her at the door of the small veterinary hospital, his ever-present battered hat pulled down over his thinning gray hair, his time-worn, lined face hidden in the shadows, his satchel in hand, when Kate had pulled up at six thirty that morning.

Kate had driven through the darkness with her new boss at her side. The mountain cold was numbing, and her sheepskin-lined jacket, pulled snug around her slender frame, gave little protection against the harsh Virginia wind. With gloved hands she had held tightly to the steering wheel, feeling every bounce as a wrenching shock up her spine. Will had sat easily on the seat next to her, balancing with the flat of his feet, his hands resting loosely on the satchel full of veterinary tools in his lap.

Kate was beginning now, this long time later, to get that same balance—as though she were firmly attached to this earth and could move with it as it spun and rolled beneath her, like a sailor born to the sea. But then, that cold dawn, she had arrived at the farm feeling as though she had been tossed in a blender.

Only her pride and training had kept her from fleeing out into the hills when she saw the Guinea brood sow lying on its side. More than anything, she did not want to help this three-hundred-and-eighty-pound mama have her babies. Under duress pigs bite! But Will was looking at her, as was the farmer, who wore a very skeptical expression on his round face. So she'd done her best and her best had been damn good.

Even Will had been pleased, and he was no pushover. Kate grinned with pleasure at the memory as she stared down at Molly's dimpled, hairy skin. "And to think you were the runt of the litter," she said aloud. "Little did I know the trouble you'd be. And look at you now—" Kate applied a topical antibiotic liberally to the wound. "Got yourself in a mess of trouble now, and I don't know if I can pull you out of it. . . ." Her practiced eye could almost see the butcher's markings: chops, loin, hocks . . . "Poor old pig!"

The first tremor of returning consciousness shivered beneath the pig's skin.

"Whoa! Hold on, Molly, I'm not ready for you yet!" Over the antibiotic she began to paint a coating of foul-smelling ointment that would keep the pig from worrying the ulcer further, working as fast as her fingers would allow her. The thick, viscous cream crept beneath Kate's fingernails, coated her palms, stuck her fingers together. She sniffed in distaste as

11

the pungent smell filled her head. "Only for you, you gorgeous creature." She laughed aloud. "My, what trouble children can be!"

A low male laugh rumbled through the small operating room.

Startled, Kate spun around toward the sound. A man was leaning in the doorway, one broad shoulder angled against the frame. The instant of fear was replaced, almost immediately, by another, far more pleasant emotion.

He was very good to look at, this stranger, with a stark, rough-hewn handsomeness that Kate found immensely appealing,

She was having the same effect on his startled sensibilities. This was not what he had expected to find, this woman with storm-dark hair and skin like dawn, tinted with rose and amber. And although her movements had the grace and ease of a thoroughbred, her spirit shone as winsome as a colt's. He had already memorized her smile, the clear ring of her laughter.

"Prettiest thing I ever did see," he said softly. A teasing, crooked smile played over his lips, and his eyes smiled into hers.

Kate saw blue eyes. Deep and clear as the sky over the ridge on an April morning. Sky-blue eyes edged with fine lines at the corners, lines that spoke of laughter or of looking long into far-distant places. Eyes to get lost in. And a strong jaw, prominent cheekbones. The angles of his face were softened by the full, generous mouth.

It was the arrogant smile that shook Kate back to

12

reality. One dark, winged brow flew up, creasing her smooth forehead. "What? I beg your pardon!"

"Damn pretty sight," he repeated, his eyes lingering on her face, then brushing slowly over her throat, the fullness of her breasts, the slimness of her tall body hidden beneath the surgical smock.

For a brief moment Kate felt bare, undressed, exposed. "Now just you wait a moment!"

He straightened and, still grinning, took a step toward her. He was tall, she realized. Tall and lean, dressed in light slacks, the sleeves of his shirt rolled to the elbow, his jacket slung over his shoulder. His body showed well in his clothes—broad shoulders, slim hips, long legs. She was a tall woman, five foot eight in her bare feet, and he stood four or five inches over her height, smiling down with that devilish grin. "Well, I always *was* fond of pigs."

Kate's eyes widened, but before she could answer, he continued with maddening nonchalance.

"That's one hefty little pig you've got there. What's his problem?"

She was glad for any excuse to pull her eyes away from his hypnotic glance. He was blatantly teasing her and now had managed to shift the conversation before she could give him the comeuppance he deserved. Ignoring the pounding of her blood through her veins, she answered coolly, "Ulcerated laceration. And as you can plainly see, I am right in the middle of a procedure. Please leave. Visitors and salesmen are not allowed in surgery." In chilly dismissal she turned her attention back to the uncon-

13

scious pig, her ears listening for the telltale click of the door. None came. She glared up from beneath the thick fringe of her lashes.

"Sir. There is a waiting room right back through the door behind you. For waiting! And a receptionist I'm surprised ever let you in here in the first place!"

"Who . . . Arie? Well, no one was at the desk," he said, shrugging. Then his brows drew together and the smile vanished from his lips. "I have one question for you. What are you doing in the old man's operatory?"

Kate's voice was cold, stiff with injured loyalty. "If you are referring to Dr. Turner, I'd advise you to show some proper respect. And as for my being here —this is *my* afternoon for surgery."

"Then nothing's wrong?"

"The only thing wrong is that you are keeping me from my work. And I've had quite enough of your interruption, Mr. . . . Mr. . . . whoever you are!"

His eyes narrowed until the blue seemed darker, piercing. He stepped closer, rested both elbows on the surgical cabinet just to her left, and leaned across it toward her. That amused smile was back on his lips. "You don't know who I am?"

For the briefest second, something flickered across her brain—a tickle of recognition. Then it fled, replaced by indignation. "No! And I don't think I want to!"

"But *I* want to know who *you* are. That's why I came on in, instead of behaving myself and waiting

14

outside. That first glimpse of you lured me. But I wanted a closer look at you, whoever *you* are."

"I am Dr. Harrington, Dr. Turner's associate. And you must be the rudest, most impossible salesman I've ever met. No wonder you've got this territory. Keep it up and you'll be peddling horse vitamins in Podunk!"

"Maybe." He winked, and his lips parted in a wicked smile. "Then again, maybe not. But right now I think you've got problems other than my future on your hands."

He pointed a warning finger down at the operating table between them. Kate dropped a cautious glance in that direction. Molly was staring up at her through one bloodshot eye!

Kate jumped. The pig grunted. Then all hell broke loose! Molly gathered her short little legs under her, shook herself furiously, showering everything within a six-foot radius with droplets of sticky ointment, and lurched crazily toward the table's edge.

"Oh, no! Hold on there, girl!" Kate yelped, her attention now riveted on the writhing bundle of pig skittering across the slick tabletop. Kate wrapped her arms around the pig, but its sideways momentum caught her full in the chest, threw her off balance, and sent them both tumbling to the floor.

"Ow! Take it easy now." Kate tried to calm the frightened animal, who was squealing rather like the proverbial stuck pig. "Easy now . . . Oh, no . . ."

Then the stranger was on the floor beside her, one arm curving under her arm, sliding protectively be-

15

tween her and the pig. In the midst of the chaos Kate was aware of the warmth of his bare skin penetrating the thin cotton of her smock, brushing against her breasts. His other hand held his jacket firmly over the pig's head, and the hooding effect had stilled Molly's struggles.

"Now what?" he asked with a nervous laugh.

"Can you hold her for a moment by yourself? I'll get a syringe—"

"Wait. I'm closer. Let me just reach up here . . ." He rocked back on his heels, felt quickly along the shelf, and brought down the syringe. With practiced ease he flicked the cap off with his thumb and handed her the injection of anesthetic.

Kate squirted half into the air, then plunged the remainder into Molly's thick hide. In moments the pig was asleep again, looking as peaceful as pork pie.

Kate let her breath out slowly. "Thank you!" She looked across at the stranger, feeling a shared warmth. "You were . . ." She bit her lip to suppress a rising tide of bubbling laughter. "You were really a . . . help—" Then a laugh burst through her words, and she was immediately joined by his deep, husky chuckling.

"Look at you," Kate choked. "You are absolutely covered with ointment."

His laughter was rich and mellow. "Then we make a good pair, Dr. Harrington, you and I." He stroked a blunt forefinger across her cheek and showed her the result. "That doesn't look like apricot facial—"

"And your shirt—"

16

"And your smock." His warm fingers toyed with the collar of her once-white surgical top. Again she felt the warmth of his presence, and her laughter became edged with caution. She began to draw away, but his fingers lingered there against her skin. "You are one beautiful lady, Dr. Harrington. And I'd like to get to know you better—without that smock."

Kate pulled away. "I do have work to finish . . . and you—"

"I'm to go wait in the waiting room, right?"

"Yes." Then softer, "Please?"

"Okay. But don't I get another thank-you first?"

"What? It was all *your* fault to begin with!"

"Ah, I had hoped you'd forgotten. But"—his broad shoulders lifted in a shrug—"I'll be seeing you again." He turned and walked to the door.

Kate's voice stopped him in midstride. "Listen, I could talk to you later . . . when I get this cleaned up, about . . . whatever your line is."

That smile tugged at the corner of his mouth. "Maybe I'd better work on my line a bit first." And he was gone.

After a brisk, well-deserved shower in the back bath at the clinic, Kate slipped into a pair of tailored gray pants and a matching blouse, ran a brush through her thick black hair, and closed up the clinic for the day. She was exhausted and wanted to rest her slender, weary frame in one of Will's overstuffed chairs and put the day's events behind her. And perhaps Arie had even built a fire in the cozy den. She'd

17

just run into town to pick up a few things at the drugstore, then she'd relax awhile.

But it was now nearly the dinner hour when she finished her errands, and Kate hurried along the narrow sidewalk lining the town's main street. A beautiful sunset lit her path, bathing the mountain ridges, shops, and clusters of white homes in a soft, hazy red glow. The natural light illuminated the signs fronting the stores along her pathway—names that had graced these businesses for many generations: Jamieson's Department Store, Benson's Antiques, Tucker's Café. The usual group of octogenarians lined the freshly painted porch of the market, idling in the ancient oak rockers that their fathers had sat in before them.

As Kate passed, they smiled and tipped their worn hats. Then the graying heads bent once again in unison as they resumed their daily philosophizing. Dr. Kate was already well known in the small town and surrounding environs. This young woman with the smoke-black hair and willowy body, full of calm movements and sureness; a country-looking girl, as though she had been raised in these parts, though it was not so. Born to money in Philadelphia, Kate had been reared and educated in the finest northeastern tradition. But her spirits had sought wider realms, and she had slipped into this newly chosen life with ease. Not infrequently she was seen late at night rumbling through the town in her Land Rover on her way to monitor a feeble cow's birthing or to care for an ill foal. The townsfolk now knew her as a friend, although they could never quite understand why she had chosen them . . . and Hickory Ridge.

But to Kate Harrington it was as clear as the morning dew on the rosebay buds outside her cabin doorway. The honesty of the people. The freshness of the rich land. The spaciousness and freedom to be herself. Not only did these add a needed dimension to her veterinary work, but also they added peace and purpose to her very life. Here, in these Blue Ridge Mountains, she felt for the first time that she could truly shape her own future.

Her Philadelphia friends and family had scoffed and argued and finally shrugged their shoulders in defeat. "She'll get it out of her system and come home," her parents had explained, smiling indulgently at their headstrong daughter.

But to Kate, these deep valleys and tree-covered slopes *were* home.

And now it was almost dinnertime. Kate quickened her pace. Aunt Arie would be waiting, and one did not keep Arie waiting long. Kate looked forward to dinner with Will and his sister. Perhaps it would help relieve the uneasiness she felt, calm the unexplainable quickening within her. She found her eyes moving in and out of store windows along the now-shaded street, seeking a glimpse of the stranger who had so abruptly dropped onto the scene and then disappeared. A salesman—that was the only logical explanation—a salesman, and not a very good one at that! Didn't have the patience to wait until she was finished or until Arie returned. Yet, she thought musingly, he didn't *look* like a salesman. How silly! What did a salesman look like, anyway? And why was she so bothered that he didn't stay around? Yet, try as she might, she could not erase that crooked smile, the amused glint in the piercing deep blue eyes, the sensuous curve of his lips, and the sound of his voice. It's hunger, she thought, placing a tanned hand across her flat abdomen. That's what it is. She laughed, forcing the handsome stranger out of her thoughts, yet somewhere admitting that he had inspired a hunger of a very special kind.

Will's home was adjacent to the clinic, connected by a small brick walkway and nestled back in a grove of shade trees. It was a comfortable home, peppered with family mementos and pictures of Will's late wife, Etta, but without superfluous amenities. Those that Arie had managed to sneak in—vases of flowers, brilliant throw rugs, and colorful oils done by local artists—went outwardly unnoticed by the frugal man, but Kate and Arie both knew the added warmth was silently appreciated. Will was not frugal in a distasteful way. He owned enough land throughout the hills to buy and sell anyone in town or even the town itself. It was simply that there was little in the world that he considered worth buying.

Kate smiled as she thought of the grumbling old vet she had grown so fond of over the past months. *Yes*, she thought, satisfied, *this is where I belong*.

She rounded the back corner of the house, which was edged with a lush hedge of forsythia, and slipped through the screened door into the welcoming, delicious aromas of Aunt Arie's kitchen. A heavy, round oak table filled the center of the cheery room, and shiny brass utensils hung from hooks and racks along the flowery, papered walls. Freshly washed curtains softened, just noticeably, the sun's retreating light, and the rays rested comfortably on Aunt Arie's familiar white head.

At the light sound of Kate's footsteps on the patterned linoleum floor Arie paused before the stove and turned from her steaming kettle. " 'Bout time. Now sit yourself down here, Kate, and calm those growls I hear comin' from your stomach before we all go deaf!" She kissed Kate's forehead lightly, and in one smooth movement had placed a basket of hot, fried biscuits and a mug of apple butter before her.

Kate grinned and, as one always did, followed Aunt Arie's directives, settling herself in the cushioned chair and smothering a hot roll with the thick, amber-colored butter. "Hm-m-m. Aunt Arie, what was life like before you? How did I ever manage?" She savored the sweet taste on her lips as she watched the older woman move expertly about the kitchen.

"Sometimes I wonder that myself!" Arie's glance swept over her. "It takes more to feed you than two farmhands—and there you are, not bigger than a wisp around the middle. I don't know, Kate Harrington, I don't know . . . maybe it's not *food* you're missin'."

Kate shot her a quick glance. She had heard this conversation before and was definitely not up to it tonight. "Oh, no, you don't, Arie Turner! I'm well aware that the Wilcotts' oldest son is in town for three weeks, is unattached, and is quite a success in the state capital. *And* I know that the new teacher at the high school is thirty-one, handsome, and 'the steady type.' But no . . . please . . . tonight is not the time."

Arie took the cue and fell into idle chatter, but her voice was clear and caring. She worried about Kate just as she worried about Will, and she was not about to let Kate deter her in her quest to find roots for the lovely twenty-seven-year-old woman.

"Well, Kate Harrington, if I can't find you a man, at least I can try to plump you up a bit. Skin and bones, girl. If it's the last thing Arie does, it'll be to put some meat on you!"

Kate laughed and popped another biscuit into her mouth, then licked the thick butter off her fingers. "Anything you say, Aunt Arie . . ."

"Gracious!" Arie glanced at the clock hanging above her stove. "Now where could Will be? It's nearly time to serve. . . ." Following the routine set up for her nearly fifty years before, Arie served dinner at six o'clock each evening—six o'clock sharp, not a moment sooner or later. And more often than not, Will missed it completely, or shook off his boots at the back door, muddy from helping a farmer drag a sick cow through the pasture, and folded his weary body into the chair just as Arie began serving dessert. And each time his sister magically produced a steaming hot meal from the belly of her kitchen, each time scolding him and warning that it was the last time.

22

"I haven't seen him all afternoon, Arie. He was going out to Richardson's farm to check on the new calves but said he'd be back by dinner—"

"Yes, yes! So he says. No sense of timing about him at all, that man. Leaves you all alone in the clinic with sick pigs and what have you—"

"Speaking of sick pigs, Molly is doing just fine. She's going to be as good as new in no time at all."

Arie's face softened. "Oh, I'm so glad. Little Freddie just loves that pig. The boy was so terribly upset that I took him along home for a while while you were operating before his pa picked him up. Gave him some of my peanut butter cookies he loves so—"

"Oh, so that's where you were when the salesman came in—"

"Salesman? Weren't any salesmen in today, Kate."

"Well, some man came into the operatory while I was working on Molly." Kate felt a hot blush coat her neck and creep up toward her face. The thought of the stranger was electrifying, and Kate tingled with the disturbing sensations that flooded her. "He was looking for the Doc but left before I had a chance to find out what he wanted. He . . . he knew you were usually at the desk—called you by name—so I presumed he had been here before. But I don't think it's been since I've been here."

Arie's thin, gray brows drew together. "Funny, we weren't expecting any salesmen. Knew me? Hmm-m-m. What did you say he looked like, Kate?"

Kate laughed uncomfortably. "Well, I don't know exactly . . ." But *exactly* she did know—remembered every line of the strong back, the hard muscles beneath the thin shirt. And the sharp eyes, sparkling and clear, laughing into her own as his tanned skin brushed against hers. "He . . . he was about six foot three, I guess, maybe in his early thirties. You know, Aunt Arie"—Kate brushed a loose strand of hair behind one ear—"like a salesman. Although . . . although I have to admit he was a lot better looking than most that come through here. Very handsome— in a rough sort of way."

Arie shot her a sideways glance. "Strange he pushed his way into the back part of the clinic. My salesmen don't usually get so uppity."

"Well, that's what I thought, too, but . . ." Kate pushed her chair back and stood up. "Oh, Arie, just forget I mentioned it. If he has anything worthwhile to sell, he'll be back!" She laughed lightly, removed a handful of silverware from the drawer, and moved into the dining room to set the table, casting all thoughts of the mysterious stranger out the open window and feigning a calm she definitely didn't feel.

The grinding wheels of Will's pickup screeched to a stop in the drive just as Arie and Kate set the steaming bowls of beef stew on the table. His booming voice greeted them as he tugged his boots off outside the door, washed his hands in the kitchen sink, then eased his tired body into the chair at the head of the table.

The country doctor's weathered hands rested on the white tablecloth, the years of hard toil and dedication etched into the wrinkled crevices. Kate's eyes lingered on his face. The tiny wrinkles about his eyes fanned out until they crossed over those traveling down from his forehead and up from his thin cheeks. His face reminded her of a finely carved statue, worn by time's relentless hand, and Kate was unexpectedly moved by a fleeting awareness of mortality.

"Well, come on, you two! It all tastes much better if you put it into your mouth!" Arie broke the silence and Will immediately looked up, then placed his hand briefly on top of Kate's in an infrequent show of affection. "Guess we had better listen to the old biddy, Kate." He winked.

Kate smiled, and in minutes, the three were enjoying the rich stew, thick with hunks of beef and vegetables. It was accompanied with hot biscuits and a colorful salad from Arie and Will's backyard garden.

"Now, Will Turner," Arie spoke up. "Tell us about the new dairy farm down at Hucker's place."

Will looked up and answered readily. "Too many gadgets! Kill the whole herd of cows if they don't watch their step with those damn computer milkers!"

Arie and Kate laughed at the man's grumblings, knowing that Will was cautious, but that he was the first to adapt to anything that was proven safe and for the betterment of his animals. Once he understood the computers, he'd be urging all his clients to sign up.

"Speaking of gadgets, Will, Kate tells me there was

a salesman hanging around here today. Have you been fussing with my books? You order something you didn't tell me about?"

" 'Course not, Arie. You know I wouldn't touch your books with a ten-foot pole." Mistakes were made in this life, but *never* in Arie's financial records. And the whole staff, including Will, approached them with papal reverence. "Couldn't've been a salesman. Not the right time of the month. Must have been a mistake. Probably some fool lost his way on the curlicued freeway exit they put in over the ridge, and was looking for directions."

Kate felt the now-familiar twist in her stomach, the rapid pulsing of her heart. She felt suddenly exposed —and guilty—but she didn't know of what. She could feel the redness in her cheeks and avoided looking directly into Will's eyes. "Well, Doc, maybe so, but he seemed to know his way around . . . even knew something about instruments and where they were kept. And he asked for you personally."

Will's eyebrows shot up. Then he seemed to take a deep breath and his face relaxed. "Nope." Will's voice was slow and deliberate. "Must've been no one, that's who. No one at all." His gaze moved from Kate to Arie, then settled on the kitchen door. "Now, sister of mine, where's that apple pie I smelled all the way from Richardson's place? And I pray to the Lord it doesn't have any of those dagnabbit seeds in it that stick in my teeth!"

Kate switched off the overhead light, plunging the bedroom of the cabin into shadowy twilight. The circling woods seemed suddenly nearer, as if they had taken a giant stride toward the small structure perched in their midst. For Kate it was a welcome embrace. She felt safe here. At peace. The scurryings and hurryings of the mice, coons, and foxes were gentle music to her ears. The rushings and shushings of the wind through the thinning leaves on the branches were a lullaby. Clad in her nightgown, a pale, ivory shift of fine cotton and lace, she stepped to the window and threw it open to the dusk. "Night silence is deepest," she whispered to the night as the breeze stirred her hair and her gown. Black hair as dark as the shadows caught in the arms of the pines and cedars hugging the window. Gown and skin as fair and translucent as the elf-light her neighbors spoke of with awe. Resting her elbows on the sill, she leaned out into the twilight. Her hair spilled loosely about her face; her dark eyes glowed. For now she was not Dr. Kate—not Katherine Harrington, DVM, but Katherine of the woods. It was an old fantasy—a dearly held dream. And it had come true.

When she had first arrived in Hickory Ridge, Arie had suggested she use the Turner mountain cabin, fifteen miles from town, sitting at the end of a curving road up into the hills. The idea had intrigued her, but Will had immediately poo-pooed the suggestion. "Sending a city girl up into these mountains . . . What's gotten into your head, Arie? Filled with cotton, I'd say!"

But Arie had driven her up, anyway, and Kate had fallen in love with the cabin immediately. It was perfect. The thick hand-hewn logs and stone were fitted together more tightly than the bricks in the spacious colonial home in which Kate had been reared. The warm, inviting living room beckoned her, and she knew this was where she had to stay. An oversize stone fireplace, lined on either side by floor-to-ceiling bookcases, filled one wall. Comfortable love seats covered in tasteful burgundy and blue prints formed a cozy area in front of the fire, drawn together by a thick braided rug. An old oak desk filled the niche created by the bay windows, and everywhere were pictures and lovely old vases and hundreds of books.

A mellow radiance suffused the mountain hideaway, and Kate often found herself wondering about the woman who had so lovingly decorated it. Arie had explained that Will had lived there with his wife Etta until she died nearly a decade ago. Truly a wonderful lady, Arie had said. And Kate felt the right to agree, having become acquainted with her through the cabin in which she now lived.

Just then, the high clear note of a mockingbird pierced through the stillness, its song echoing on the breeze as the plain little bird sang of all the beauty it had heard that day, a blending of the world's varied music. Kate shivered. Melancholy washed over her, a longing for something glimpsed and gone. "Oh, what's bothering me?" she mused aloud. All evening she had felt a strange stirring deep within her. She pressed her fingers to the hollow of her throat, then shook her head. Perhaps it was the talk over dinner. Will's strange moments of quiet and the shadows she glimpsed behind his eyes. Perhaps she was just tired. No. The truth had something to do with the tall, sandy-haired man with the sky-blue eyes. How silly! she chided herself. That's what you get for being such an incurable romantic beneath all your calm practicality. The stranger's appearance—and sudden disappearance—had disrupted the calm surface of her routine. And like ripples on a lake, the vibrations still echoed within her. The bottomless depth of those blue eyes, the curve of his lips, the way his hair curled against his neck, the suggestion of power beneath those loose-fitting clothes . . . "Kate, stop. What's one good-looking man more or less?" she asked aloud.

A chill coursed through her body, and she ran her hands up and down her arms to chase it away. Thoughts, begone! Enough! She slapped a palm against the windowsill, startling the little birds outside into silence and bringing Ginger, her golden retriever, loping to her side. Kate knelt and rubbed the dog's silky head. "What do you say, old girl? Think I need a good dose of Aunt Arie's rose petal tea to settle my system?"

She padded barefoot into the kitchen and returned with a steaming cupful liberally laced with Walker McCoy's clover honey. "M-m-m, that's better." She settled into bed, switched on the small reading lamp above her, and tucked her toes under Ginger's warm fur. Cup in one hand, volume seventy-six of the

Belleweather, the University of Pennsylvania's Veterinary journal in the other, her thoughts turned back to reality. Veterinary medicine fascinated her, which explained her strong, youthful rebellion against her father's wishes that she go to medical school and join his pediatric practice. Even at eighteen she had stood her ground, sent her application in to veterinary school, and traveled her own road. And tonight she quickly lost herself in a fascinating article related to her field. Later, when darkness pressed against the window and her empty teacup rested on the bedcovers next to her knee, she yawned and slipped a bookmark into the heavy volume.

Suddenly Ginger lifted her head, her ears rotating back and forth like radar. Kate dropped a soothing hand on her wet nose, but the dog nudged her away. A low growl began in her throat. The alert ears pricked forward as though straining to catch a sound beyond the bedroom door. Her growl deepened. The hair rose along her back. Kate felt an answering prickle along her own spine. "What is it, girl?" She could hear nothing, but the dog had begun to intersperse her growls with a high-pitched, nervous whine. Kate slipped quickly from the bed. "What do you hear, Ginger?" She reached for the heavy flashlight she kept within easy reach in case of storms and wrapped her fingers in Ginger's fur. "Hush a minute, girl!" A sharp barb of fear stabbed at her heart. And she heard it now: the sounds the dog's keen ears had intercepted earlier. Footsteps. The cracking of twigs and rustling of leaves carried clear through the open windows. Footsteps coming from around the front of the house. Will? No, not without helloing from the jeep first. Matt Darrow bringing wood? Not this late. Then who? Yet the steps were loud, undisguised, and someone was humming softly to himself.

Tightening her grip on flashlight and fur, she pushed away her fear and stepped noiselessly across the front room and paused at the door. The knob rattled. Kate flicked on the flashlight, hissed at Ginger a command to stay, and flung open the door.

The man outside yelped in surprise, threw his arm up to shield his eyes from the flashlight's blinding glare, and cursed loudly. "What the hell! Who's there? Put down that damn thing, would you!"

It was the stranger from that afternoon.

Kate's jaw dropped open and she stared at him. His slacks were mud-spattered, his jacket covered with the fine dust of dry leaves, his thick, fair hair tousled. Had he followed her home? But how? Why?

"Hey, will you cut that light?"

"Yes. But stay where you are. Don't move!" Kate redirected the flashlight's beam but maintained a firm grip on its heavy weight. Ginger's bare teeth gleamed white.

Now it was his turn to stare openmouthed. "You?"

His surprise was obviously genuine. But if he had not followed her . . . "What are you doing here?" she asked, finding her voice.

"I was just going to ask you the same thing," he answered. He shifted his weight, thrusting his hands into his pockets as the beginnings of a grin touched

31

his mouth. Ginger growled at the movement and the man froze. "Hey, take it easy." He glanced uneasily from the dog to Kate. "You don't understand."

"You bet I don't! All I know is that you've shown up twice today . . . in very unlikely places, at two very inappropriate times. You've got some explaining to do, mister—and fast."

He held her eyes and stood silent a moment, watching her as if weighing her words, her presence. His eyes held amusement, admiration—and something else. "Could I come in . . . to explain?"

"I wouldn't try it!"

"Ah." He smiled. "Well, I'm Craig—"

"Well, Mr. Craig—"

"No, not *Mr.* Craig. Craig Turner. I'm Will Turner's son."

It took Kate a moment to comprehend his words. Then she could see the truth written in his features. The resemblance that had touched that unconscious part of her brain earlier today. The tawny brows, the long straight nose, the angle of his jaw, the wide, generous mouth. She had only known Will as an old man, his features set in grim determination, his shoulders stooped by work and age. And this man was young and alive and virile, exuding a lean, hard strength. Could he be telling the truth?

"I . . . I didn't know Will *had* a son!"

The young man's laughter was edged with pain, and a telltale muscle jumped along his jaw. "Yes . . . I'd bet he didn't mention the fact."

"But I told Will you had been to the office. I mean, I described you," she objected, even more puzzled.

"I haven't seen my father in over four years, and"—his voice grew tight—"he never did see me . . . even then."

"But I thought you were a salesman. You knew that, and never corrected me."

"You didn't give me much chance, remember? And you don't believe me now, even when you're standing in *my* door, in *my* house, to which I still hold the key. See?" The metallic gleam of the key flashed golden in his palm. "Now, may I come in . . . please?"

"I suppose so. Yes." Kate stepped back from the doorway, dragging a reluctant Ginger with her. "It's all right, girl." She laid a hand on Craig's arm as she spoke. "It's okay. . . ." Without moving her hand she looked up into those electric blue eyes, her own dark eyes flashing. "I'd better be right, Mr. Turner, or Ginger will gobble you up in one quick bite!"

His lips twitched in amusement. "It's all right. I'm safe."

Kate cast a suspicious glance at the handsome, rugged face. "*That* I doubt. But you had better behave."

He followed her into the house, his eyes lingering for a moment on the very visible curves of Kate's graceful body. And then his gaze wandered fondly over the interior of the small front room, resting on the cotton cambric curtains, the old pewter candlesticks on the mantelpiece, the faded landscapes in their narrow frames on the walls. When he dropped

33

down into the soft cushions at the far end of the couch, his hand brushed lovingly over its familiar pattern. A shadow of memory darkened his eyes. And Kate felt uncomfortably like the intruder.

She cleared her throat, and his gaze turned obediently back to her face. "Why . . . why didn't Will ever tell me about you?"

"You mean you and the old man actually talk?" He pushed his fingers through his thick hair. "You must be a magician"—he cocked one brow and peered closer into her eyes—"or a spellbinder. That's the right word!"

Kate's discomfort was acutely heightened, as was her awareness of his being near. "Nothing of the sort. I simply like Will, that's all. We get along fine." She stood and headed for the kitchen. "I think I need a cup of coffee and a bit of something. Can't handle all this on an empty stomach. May I get you something?"

"No. Nothing, thanks."

"Okay. Here, Ginger—come, girl."

But the dog only lifted her head and lay where she had settled near Craig's feet. Instinctively the animal seemed to know Craig belonged here. "Some watchdog you are!"

"He's got good taste, that's all."

"She. A veterinarian's son should be able to tell the difference."

"Right. But I wasn't looking at her. . . ." He winked and grinned at her across the room.

Kate felt not only his proximity but also her own

34

nakedness. Her unbound breasts and loins under the thin shift of her nightgown. The delicacy of the gown itself. "Well, I'm sure there's plenty here in this room to stir old memories for you, and—"

"I was looking at you."

His bluntness unnerved her totally.

"You are very beautiful," he persisted, his eyes never leaving her.

Her breasts rose with the quick intake of her breath. "I . . . I'm going to get that coffee. Ginger, come along. Ginger? Okay then, stay where you are!" And with a shrug she turned and fled into the kitchen, snatched an old cardigan sweater from a hook near the back door, and buttoned it protectively from hem to throat. She knew he was watching her with that maddening smile, those sexy, midnight-blue eyes. She banged the refrigerator door open and closed, yanked out a couple of drawers, and kicked at the stove. Then she began to feel better. Back in control. When she emerged a few minutes later, a hefty slice of Aunt Arie's boysenberry pie on a plate in one hand, coffee in the other, her composure had settled snugly back in place. For the moment.

"There you are." His voice was honey. "I missed you."

"I can understand why. I'm fascinating company." She lowered her slender frame into the protective arms of the leather wingback chair near the fireplace and balanced her snack on her lap. "There. Now. Back to the question at hand. How do—"

"The question at hand? You sound more like a lawyer than a country vet. How did my father find you, anyway?"

"*That* is not the question, Mr. Turner. This evening I'm the interviewer—and you're the interviewee!" Her dark eyes sparkled as she struggled to keep the laughter out of her voice. "I ask the questions and you answer them. Or it's out you go—and it is getting mighty nippy out there. Now, question number one: How do I know you *are* Craig Turner? You could be telling me a story, feeding me that line we spoke of earlier—"

"How do I prove I'm Craig Turner?" His broad shoulders curved forward as he leaned his elbows on his knees and stared down into his lap for a moment, seemingly lost in serious thought. Then his face creased into a mischievous grin as he snapped his fingers. "I've got it! I haven't had to use this in a long time, but—" He rose, stretched to his full height, and came to stand dangerously close to Kate. His fingers worked swiftly at his belt buckle, and in seconds, the belt lay like a snake across her knees. "You see"—he grinned down at her—"I have this foolproof, identifying birthmark. . . ."

Kate's round, wide eyes shot to his waist, disbelieving. "No . . . no! Don't you dare!"

"I was only about to—" he began innocently.

"I *know* what you were about! And I'm not having any of it! Sit back down there." She pointed shakily at the couch, a safe four feet away.

"Yes, ma'am." But then, as though it were the most

36

natural thing in the world, he bent, lifted the pie plate from her lap, and took an enormous bite.

"That's *my* pie!"

"No it isn't," he mumbled through a mouthful of pie, then swallowed. "It's Aunt Arie's. I'd recognize the taste anywhere. But here, I'm a good guy. I'll share." And curving down over her, so close that she could smell the subtle musk of his scent, he cut a forkful and slid it between her lips.

For a second, she was stunned with surprise. Then her teeth snapped shut on the fork's metallic surface. But it was too late. Glaring at him, she succumbed to the only available option and swallowed the sweet morsel. She ran the tip of her tongue over her lips. "Are you always this . . . this . . ." She groped for the right word, trying desperately to calm the rising tide of her excitement, and her thoughts failed her.

"Generous?" he rasped sexily. "No. Only when I come home to find a raven-haired beauty waiting at my door. On the inside!"

Kate tried hopelessly to catch hold of the unraveling threads of her vanishing self-control. "Mr. Turner. I want you to go sit back down there and finish your pie . . . and . . ."

"I always finish what I've started." He grinned.

Kate ignored his latest interruption and pointed a commanding finger at the couch. "Sit!"

Ginger's ears perked up. Craig turned soulful eyes in the dog's direction. "Don't worry, old girl—that was for me." And he sat, elbows on knees, the sinewy muscles of his forearms lying like ropes beneath the skin, the skin itself covered with light golden hair in the lamplight.

Kate tore her eyes away. "All right now. Next question." Her voice escaped, trembling through a tight throat. "What *are* you doing up here at this time of night?"

"I was planning on sleeping here."

"You were what?"

"I was coming home. Going to bed. Why look so surprised?"

"Because I . . . I . . . well, I didn't think about that. And you can't! *I* sleep here."

"There are two bedrooms. And a couch."

"Oh, no! I don't know where you've spent the last four years, but women do not invite strange men to spend the night in Hickory Ridge."

"Do men let strange women spend the night in *their* homes in Hickory Ridge?"

"You wouldn't—"

One tawny brow climbed high above suddenly gentle blue eyes. "No. You're right. I wouldn't. But I don't have many alternatives myself."

"Listen." Kate leapt to her feet, and she clattered the cup and saucer onto the small end table that held the phone. "I've got an idea! Why not call Will now?" She lifted the receiver and held it out to him. "Tell him you're here, and I can run you down into town—"

"No, Kate." He shook his head and covered her hand with his. His fingers were cool, and she could feel rough calluses against the tips of her own fingers.

"No. Thanks but no thanks. A phone call from me would not be a surprise Will would welcome."

"But—"

"No." He said it softly without sharpness but with a firmness that silenced her. She knew immediately he was not the kind of man one could push too far.

"Then what shall we do?" she asked, dropping the phone back into its cradle. "I've got to get to bed. I'm due back at the clinic at six."

"What we both need is a good night's sleep." He smiled at her with a sudden, unnerving boyish innocence. "It has been quite a day. Come on. Two bedrooms. Two of us. No problem, right?" And he headed for the first door.

Kate darted in front of him and planted her lithe body in the door frame. "Where are you going?"

"To bed. My bed. In there—" He pointed past her into the darkness.

"Oh, no. You can't sleep here. That's *my* room."

"Ah, so you've been sleeping in *my* bed!" He spread his arms, held on to the door frame, and leaned in toward her. "Had any interesting dreams? Felt my vibes?"

"I don't want to feel your vibes! And I'm a very sound sleeper—I rarely dream."

"Too bad."

"Suits me fine. And I have another idea." She pushed the flat of one palm against the front of his shirt and pushed him out of the way. "Why don't you go get a room down at Steven's Motel? My treat—"

He shook his head, his eyes never leaving her face.

39

"Word would spread like wildfire. Prodigal sons make big news in these parts."

"Then how about friends . . . or somewhere . . ." she whispered, clinging to her last straw of hope.

"I am somewhere . . . and let's be friends." He held out his hand and smiled that irresistible smile.

CHAPTER TWO

Kate slapped blindly at the buzzing alarm and succeeded only in knocking the clock over the edge of her night table. "Oh, stop—please stop!" she groaned, pulling first pillow, then blankets over her head. The alarm's persistent cry tunneled after her, filling her aching head with its silent wail. Why did she feel as if she had just closed her eyes? This was not like her. She was most definitely a morning person, facing each dawn with hope and cheer and plans as fresh and crisp as just-baked bread. Today she felt like a stale loaf or a dried-up crumb swept under the rug. Oh, her aching head.

"Could you cut out that infernal racket!" A rough male voice filtered through the wall.

Kate's eyes popped open. A man's voice. And instantaneously she remembered, could picture quite clearly, the man to whom it belonged. Craig Turner. She expected to see him in her doorway any second. And surely would if she didn't stifle that alarm. Kate jumped from bed, pushed in the button on the back of the clock, and listened to the silence. No voice. No footsteps. Nothing. Still nervously watching the door, not knowing whether she was anticipating or dreading his appearance, she edged toward the small bathroom that separated the two bedrooms. She knocked first very softly. "Hello? Good morning. Are you in there?" Nothing. Gingerly she turned the knob and peeked in. Empty. In a flash she had crossed the cold tile floor, the chill pulling all of her sleepy warmth out through the bottom of her bare feet, and snapped the lock on the adjoining door. Safe! For the time being.

She showered and washed her thick shoulder-length hair in record time, speed worthy of the *Guinness Book of World Records,* she was sure. There were still soap bubbles clinging to her breasts and the smooth curve of her belly as she rubbed herself dry with the enormous, white terry towels Etta Turner had stocked the linen closet with years ago. No monograms. No designer colors. Just plain and simple and heavenly on a cold mountain morning. Kate stopped. The towel hung loosely in one hand, her wet ebony hair still plastered to neck and cheek. Etta Turner. That was Craig's mother. Her brows drew together in a straight, dark line. How strange to think of that. Will and Etta, young and in love. Craig, their son. And Aunt Arie, *really* someone's aunt. How amazing! How amazing that it was real now, when before yesterday none of it had existed for her. Today it seemed suddenly very important. There was Craig Turner, asleep just beyond the door.

She glanced from door to mirror, an impish grin curving her lips. How did he see her? she wondered. Lifting the wet hair from her neck, she turned slowly before the mirror, first one way, then the other. Well, it was no model's body, that was for sure. No boyish, flat little chest: Her breasts were full and tipped with pert, rosy nipples. Her hips curved sensuously, but she had a narrow waist and good long legs. And her skin, glowing now from her toweling, was sleek and smooth as a deer's. A good body, she declared approvingly to the girl in the mirror, then laughed behind her hand, hoping she hadn't spoken aloud. With a wink, she wrapped the towel around her, stepped back into her bedroom, and firmly locked the door.

The alarm had sounded at four thirty, and by five fifteen Kate was dressed in fawn-colored slacks and an argyle sweater patterned in soft, muted hues. Apron-clad, she was frying pancakes at the old two-burner stove in the kitchen. Atop her pancakes, their faces pleasingly browned by the hot skillet, she ladled applesauce, raisins, and chopped walnuts. "Down!" she whispered commandingly to Ginger as the dog's wistful nose appeared over the edge of the table. "No, girl—go eat your Kibbles, poor baby." For herself she sliced an orange, poached an egg, poured a steaming cup of coffee, and sat down to breakfast.

43

"My God! Are you expecting Attila the Hun? Or merely the entire Eighth Infantry?"

Her heart stopped.

Craig stood in the doorway. He was wearing his slacks, socks but no shoes, and a T-shirt. The thin white cotton stretched tightly over the smooth muscles of his shoulders, across the muscled wall of his chest. A few hairs, surprisingly dark, curled over the neck band toward his throat. He was leaning against the door frame, arms akimbo, and his skin was tanned and dark against the stark white of his shirt, smooth and warm looking, the way polished wood would feel beneath the palm of one's hand.

Kate felt a nervous jumping in her stomach and decided it must be hunger. She popped a forkful of pancakes into her mouth. "I always eat a good breakfast. It's the most—"

"—important meal of the day." Craig completed her sentence for her, strode across the room, and planted a kiss on Kate's forehead. "Good morning, dear." Laughing, he slipped into the space beside her at the table, his blue eyes registering the flush of emotion on Kate's face. His eyes were all sleepy and soft and smiling at her. "Sorry. Didn't mean to throw you off balance."

Kate laughed. "No, I guess I was sounding a bit maternal."

Craig leaned back and his eyes combed her body. "Maternal is definitely not the word I'd use to describe you!"

Again, she felt the rush of her blood and the spread

44

of heat through her limbs and deep within her. Her fork clattered noisily to the floor and she ducked to retrieve it.

"You're an awfully skittish young filly. What's got you so nervous?"

She could feel his eyes on her, evaluating, weighing. She ignored him, carefully shaking salt and pepper onto her egg.

"What is it?" he persisted, his voice coaxingly soft. "Once burned, twice shy?"

"*That*," Kate answered coolly, "is none of your business." And with a sharp jab she poked the prongs of her fork dead center into the yolk of her egg. "Bull's-eye," she quipped, her dark, flashing eyes meeting and holding his own.

Craig grinned and held his tongue.

Kate turned back to her breakfast, polishing off the hotcakes, the egg, and an orange. Fortified, she looked back over at her breakfast companion. His rumpled hair and lazy smile intrigued her; created a terribly warm, tingling sensation inside her. Kate was not sure exactly what to do with it, so she tried drowning it in another cup of coffee. Glancing over the rim of her cup, she asked, "May I get you something? A cup of coffee?"

"Now?"

"Now's when I'm here." She laughed. "In ten minutes I'll be on my way to work."

Craig glanced at the clock. "At five forty-five? Even the birds have sense enough not to get up this early!"

45

"Will starts the day at six o'clock."

"That's right." Craig nodded. "The old man cracks his whip and everyone jumps. I'd forgotten."

"It's his business," Kate answered calmly, refusing to apologize for Will's habits. "And as his associate, I do things his way. But I enjoy it. It gives us a chance to sort out the day's schedule and confer on cases and treatments before the calls begin. *You* know these people"—she let her arms swing in a wide arc as though to encompass the whole of the Blue Ridge Mountains—"up with the sun, and if a cow is going to birth or a horse break a leg, you can bet it'll be at some inconvenient hour."

"Don't I remember," he murmured, his eyes dark with memories. "Out of bed in the dark and downstairs at the crack of dawn, when my pals were still deep in dreams over their next trip to the fishing hole. And riding with the old man up into the hills by lantern light. And Mom . . . Mom, down in the laundry, washing up smocks and operating sheets when other moms were getting their first cup of coffee . . ."

The suddenly bitter look on his face made Kate's heart twist in pain. "But surely your mother chose the life she led. She loved your father."

"And *he* loved his work! Every damn horse and cow and pig . . . every stranger who bought ten acres and started a farm, but my mother—"

"And her, certainly!" Kate interrupted, her voice warm with feeling.

Craig looked at her, his eyes narrowed and unread-

46

able. "You'd better get going. Your ten minutes are up."

Kate glanced at the old wall clock, suddenly wishing she could hold its hands still. "Yes. You're right. I have to leave," she repeated reluctantly, but sat still.

"Listen, Kate. Don't tell the old man I'm here."

"But Craig—"

"No." He had tensed, and his knuckles showed white on his clenched hands. "Please don't. I'll be down later. If I see him in person—face-to-face—maybe this long overdue reunion will stand a chance."

"I'm sure it will, Craig. You know the old saying, 'Absence makes the heart grow fonder.'" She grinned encouragingly.

"Obviously *you* don't know the old man as well as you think you do. I'd settle for 'Out of sight, out of mind!'"

Shaking back her hair, Kate leaned her chin on her hands and looked into Craig's shadowed eyes. There was no way to read the mixture of emotions she saw there. Instead, she smiled again. "Well, good luck then. I hope it works out for both of you."

"Thanks." He grinned back, and every shadow vanished in the light of his smile. "But I'd feel better if I had a rabbit's foot to rub."

"Well"—she shrugged lightly—"I don't happen to have a rabbit's foot handy, but will *this* do?" And without a word, she slipped off her loafer, dropped her sock-covered foot on his lap, and wiggled her toes.

47

Craig sat stock-still for a moment, his eyes filled with a deep wonder. Then he reached down and slowly stroked her foot. "Thank you, Lady Luck."

Shifting into first, Kate began the drive into town. She pushed back the hood of her parka, feeling an unaccustomed warmth. The weather? Or more likely the heated racing of her own blood. She felt imbued with Craig's touch, his presence. It weighed upon her like a second, silken skin. His scent, his nearness, his smile—every fiber of her being registered his particular essence. Kate was confused by her response to him—such uncharacteristic behavior. She pushed aside her bewilderment as she stepped into the clinic and only the pleasure lingered.

"Good morning, Will. It promises to be another lovely day, doesn't it? Did you see that sunrise?"

"Goodness, girl! What's gotten into you? You're chatty as a magpie—"

"And you're holding your own nicely, I see," Kate replied, undaunted, her grin growing wider every minute.

"Hmpff!" Will scowled.

"That's an interesting way to end a conversation," Kate teased, hanging up her jacket and donning her white smock, knowing full well that Will would *never* let her get in the last word.

Sure enough, he planted his hands on his hips, and glared at her. "Some conversations don't need endin'. They need forgetting!"

"Yes, but—"

"And this is one of them!" He snatched the clipboard holding their schedule and slapped it noisily onto the stainless steel surface of the table between them. His eyes forbade answer, but his lips were twitching in an irrepressible smile.

It was so rare to see Will smile. Oh, he'd grin at her affectionate teasing or chuckle at a farmer's off-colored joke, but he hardly ever smiled. Kate had once asked Aunt Arie about it. It had been a month earlier at the lazy, tail-end of summer, and they had been drinking lemonade together in the shade of the old magnolia out back. They had been laughing at the antics of one of Arie's many cats. Arie was a tall, bony woman, hardened, herself, by a long, active life in the mountains. But her face folded easily into a heartwarming smile—and it had at Kate's question.

"Did Will ever laugh, Arie?" Kate asked, her lovely dark eyes filled with concern. "Did he ever . . . ever, well, just have fun?"

"Mercy yes, child. As a boy he was a mischief. I couldn't have wished for a better big brother. He was so often in trouble, why . . . our pa didn't have time to keep an eye on me. I got away with more than any other girl I knew. A regular tomboy I was, following Will's lead. The army straightened him up a bit, but when he came back he was still full of—well, spit and vinegar."

"Then what happened, Arie?" Kate sighed. "Sometimes I look at him—oh, not when he's working, because then he's always in command, but other

49

times. Like the other night after dinner, he seemed so sad. What happened?"

"What happened, child? Why, life happened. It got on with itself. And dragged him—me, too, mind you —right along with it. That's the way of things. What you've got today—happiness or sadness, poverty or plenty—is not necessarily what you'll have to-morrow."

"I know, Arie. But that's not what I mean. I'm talking about a way of looking at the world, at life. Don't you understand?"

"Even that changes, Katherine. I do understand . . . but even that changes. A happy heart can turn to stone. A dry soul burst into flower." She had gathered Kate's hand into her own, her paper-thin skin dry and cool to the touch. "And what we let slip through our fingers today, we would gladly die for tomorrow."

Kate turned her hand and entwined her fingers with Arie's, giving and receiving the reassuring pressure.

"Not me," she had answered, tossing the heavy spill of her dark hair away from her face. "I know what I want. All this is part of it . . . the clinic and Will and the mountains. Even the cows and the sheep. And the way the sun lingers at the top of the ridge at sunset. And . . . and you, Arie."

"Thank you, Kate. It's an honor to be included in such company," she teased, then said, her voice filled with surprising strength, "Just remember, Katherine. One mustn't try to hold life still. Life is not a package all neatly tied and sitting on the shelf. One's got to prick up one's ears, and stand on tiptoe to see what's coming around the corner! And don't you be worrying about Will. He's a stubborn old coot, but he has a good heart. Things will work themselves out."

Things will work themselves out! Whether they would or not was soon to be seen, Kate suspected, and the thought tugged her back to the present—the surgery, and Will's voice, sharp with exasperation.

"Heavens to Betsy, girl, you're out wool-gathering again! You and Arie have been flightier than two sheep with the wolf around the corner of the barn. Has she been feeding you that damn ginseng of hers?"

"Sorry, Will." Kate rested the back of her hand against one smooth cheek and smiled. "Don't blame Aunt Arie. I think I just need a good night's sleep." As soon as the words were out, images of the night before flashed through her mind.

She blushed and turned her face away, but Will didn't seem to notice her discomfort. Instead he quoted reproachfully, "Early to bed and early to rise . . ."

"Can make a girl quite dull!" Kate quipped, thankful for the chance to get his goat and her footing. "Now let's see here." She straightened her slender shoulders and ran the smooth oval of one nail down the paper. "What's on schedule today?" Will was heading south to Turkey Creek to poll Medson's three-year-old Herefords, while Kate was due up on the ridge at Hilary's for his annual swine inoculations. She'd be returning first to the clinic and had scheduled some small animal neuterings: a puppy and two kittens, all male and therefore all brief procedures. That would leave the surgery free for Will and his eleven o'clock operation on Mrs. Potter's poodle.

"I hate having to deal with that old biddy." He glanced at her craftily out of the corner of his eye. "If I happen to be running late, you just go ahead and take care of that, will you?"

"Don't you dare, Will! You *know* that woman will not let me lay a hand on her precious Baby. She made it quite clear to Arie that only *The Doctor* was to take care of poor Baby."

"You're the doctor, too!" Will grumped.

"Yes, but not in Mrs. Potter's eyes." Kate shook her head. "You and only you are to be awarded that honor. And now, adieu. I'm off, satchel in hand, that little old pig-sticker, me. See you later."

The sun seemed to follow her as she drove west into the mountains. Shimmering light caught in her hair and flamed there the way the sun can be seen glowing from around the edges of a dusty, billowing cloud. It warmed her shoulders and the narrow span of her back. And peeping over her shoulder like a shy friend, its rays lit the hills around her. Slanting into the dark forests it woke the sleeping birds, sent the animals tumbling from their nests and dens. Twice Kate had to stop for deer on the road, one a fawn so young it stood on trembling legs staring at the blank, looming front of the Land Rover until its mother

52

nudged it with fretful urgency and sent it skittering into the dry leaves.

Unbidden, a great longing washed over Kate to have shared that moment with someone. And the longing gave way to surprise. No, not just someone, she had to admit, being honest with herself, but with a certain someone. A tall, sandy-haired man with sky-blue eyes. She laughed at herself. Why, you don't even know if he likes deer or sunrises or anything, she scolded silently. But somehow she was sure he did. With a shake of her head that sent her sunlit hair flying, she drove on.

At the farm the grass and hay were still wet and bent with heavy dew. Kate's pantlegs were drenched by the time she reached the sty near the barn. Abel Hilary was waiting for her at the gate. Spare of words like most of the mountain people, he spoke a quick hello, then he and his son Joseph, a big, square boy of seventeen, helped her isolate and hold the pigs. Halfway through the work, Mrs. Hilary brought warm rolls and jam and home-churned butter—and mugs of hot tea.

"Morning, Lacy."

"Morning, Dr. Kate. How's it going?"

"Right well, thank you," Kate replied, brushing her hair back from her face with the back of one hand. "How's the baby?"

Lacy smiled and patted her rounded stomach. "Kickin' up a storm. Another boy, no doubt. And me, with four sons already. I'd sure like a little girl one of these times."

53

"I'm rooting for you, Lacy." Kate's brown eyes sparkled with woman-to-woman empathy. "You've got to have a daughter to pass all these wonderful recipes on to."

"Hrmph!" Abel cleared his throat loudly. "Doctor Will drinks his tea while he works."

Kate winked at the other woman and popped a third roll into her mouth. "Time to get back to work!"

Amidst squeals and oinks and a wild splattering of mud, the rest of the inoculations were administered. Kate explained what reactions Abel should be alert for, washed up in the barn, and stopped by the house for a quick good-bye. She pulled into the clinic parking lot just at nine thirty. There were three other cars there, and the tiny waiting room was crowded and noisy. A chorus of hellos greeted the appearance of her tall, slender figure. Arie hurried from behind the receptionist's desk.

"Good morning, Dr. Harrington," she said loudly. Formality in business was one of her hallmarks. She had always insisted on it for Will as a sign of respect in front of "the clients," as she called them, and she had extended the practice to include Kate.

"Good morning, Arie," Kate replied, and stepped on into the surgery. Arie followed right behind.

"I've got your instruments all sterilized and ready. There's a supply of fresh towels in the drawer. And I relettered your name tag. It had gotten rather smudged."

"Thank you, Arie."

"And you had better watch out for Mrs. Lamb this

54

morning. She's all a-twitter, afraid her poor Jo-Jo just won't be the same."

"I'll vouch for that!" Kate laughed, and Arie's businesslike demeanor melted into loud chuckles.

"Any other news . . . or concerns?"

"Let me think. Oh, yes, Hern Douglas called about having some two-year-olds castrated."

"Goodness, Arie! I'm going to get quite a reputation. The men will be afraid to come near me with a ten-foot pole!"

"Shame on you, Kate!" Arie gasped, her chuckles turning into loud laughter. "You are full of the devil this morning," she scolded. "What are you up to, girl?"

"Me? Why nothing at all," Kate answered quickly, but she felt slightly guilty at saying so—and surprised as well. Was she acting so differently? And if so, was it because of . . . No! She pushed away the appealing image that floated to the surface of her mind and slipped into a fresh smock. "Time for business," she said aloud, and turned back to Arie. Her dark eyes met Arie's gray ones, and fell. What would Arie think if she knew her long-absent nephew had spent the night at the cabin? With a very uncomfortable shiver dancing up her spine she turned toward the operating table. "If you'll send Mrs. Lamb in . . ."

The operations went quickly—one, two, three. Only instructing and reassuring the concerned "parents" took much time. Then that, too, was done, and Kate slipped into the sparkling little washroom to clean up. Splashing water on her face, she glanced into the mirror.

Was she acting differently this morning? She looked the same. Wide, dark eyes, the pupils ringed with the thinnest band of gold. Dark brows, a trifle too full, she thought. Clear skin, though perhaps the slightest bit flushed across her cheekbones. Quickly she grabbed a towel and patted her skin dry. What foolishness! She was who she always was—who she *liked* being—and that was that!

She stepped back into the operatory just as Will stepped in through the front door.

"Hello, Dr. Turner. How did it go?"

"With a snip-snip here, and a snip-snip there, Dr. Harrington!" Will answered, tossing his hat onto the rack. "And you?"

"Planned Parenthood would be proud of me!"

They laughed together, one of those rare moments when her charm overcame his reticence.

"And now for Mrs. Potter's poodle."

"Want me to stay and assist, Dr. Turner?" Kate offered.

"I'd appreciate that, Dr. Harrington."

The entrance of Mrs. Potter, quaking poodle smothered in her arms, brought conversation to a halt. "Dr. Turner, I am so worried about poor Baby. Her precious ears are so sore again. I *don't* understand. I thought you had cleared up that nasty problem the last time I brought her in, Dr. Turner. She has suffered so much, poor dear. And we both depended on you to make everything better, but now it has gone and happened again."

"And it will keep on happening, Mrs. Potter, if you don't stop putting those damn bows around her ears. How would *you* like it if someone tied ribbons around your—"

"Perhaps I could explain the problem to Mrs. Potter while you prepare Baby for surgery," Kate interrupted, stepping quickly to the woman's side and sliding a hand under her elbow. "Let's step into the other office," she said soothingly, even as she steered the resistant form toward the door.

In an hour's time the operation was completed, and Baby was returned to the safety of her "mother's" arms. Kate busied herself cleaning and sterilizing instruments while Will grumbled over Baby's chart.

"Oh, give me a cow or a horse—animals of substance—any day!" He jabbed a pointing forefinger across the table at Kate. "You're the junior associate. *You* take care of Mrs. Potter's Baby from now on!"

"Oh, no, you don't." Kate laughed. "That's why I left Philadelphia!"

A screech from the outer office interrupted their words.

"Now, what in the world was that?" Will's hands dropped to his side, and his eyes jerked toward the door as Arie's unintelligible, excited sounds continued.

"What's gotten into that woman!"

Kate stood frozen. *She* knew what was taking place

57

in the outer office. Craig had arrived. Her face paled, and she braced herself for Will's reaction.

The old man flung the door open and stopped dead in his tracks. A heavy silence fell over the room.

"Hello, Pop." Craig's voice hung on the stillness. Kate could not see his face from where she stood, but she could hear the emotion in just those two words. She *could* see Arie's face, her feelings racing across her fading features: love, dread, hope, and fear.

Then Will dropped his hand to his side, straightened, and his back filled the doorway. "You are not welcome here."

"No, Will! Don't—"

"Oh, no, Will—"

Arie and Kate's voices collided in the stillness, both women reacting instantaneously from the heart.

"This is your son."

Will stood stonelike. His eyes silenced first one, then the other. "That boy is no kin of mine."

The younger man's voice was leaden with despair. "Look at me, Dad. Talk to me. I'm no boy anymore. Won't you look at me . . . and see who I am?"

"Too late for that. Too late." And the old man turned his back, grabbed his hat, and stalked toward the rear exit. He pushed past Kate's restraining hand, and only she saw the wetness filling his eyes.

Silence hung in the room, broken only by the click of the door latch. It was Arie who spoke first.

"Craig, dear . . ." Arie reached up and held his face between her wrinkled hands, drawing his wounded gaze down to hers. "Craig, don't be hurt or angry . . . it has been so long. You shouldn't—couldn't—expect him to change. He needs time, Craig."

He patted his aunt's hand, but his voice was harsh. "I don't expect him to change. I don't expect anything. I don't know why I even bothered to come. He'll never listen to me, never talk to me. Never has. Never will." He circled her wrists with his strong, tanned hands and pulled them away from his face. "Did you hear him, Arie? I'm no son of his. That's what he said."

"But not what he meant, Craig. That old coot is my brother, and I've known him longer and better than you. That was just his anger speaking. All these years of nursing this silly feud—"

"There's no feud, Arie. It takes two to fight, and I'm not fighting. He hated me then, and he hates me now."

"You're wrong. But you, Craig, are you that innocent? I've seen that temper of yours, my dear boy." She smiled gently to soften the harshness of her words but spoke on. "The trouble is, you're too alike, you two."

"Oh, no!" Craig spun and stalked to the window. "Don't pull that old one on me! I'm *nothing* like him." He jerked a thumb toward the path outside.

Arie's eyes met Kate's frantic gaze behind the angry wall of Craig's back. The older woman smiled weakly, sensing how upset Kate was, and regretting that an outsider, however dear, should witness such an unpleasant family scene. "It will all work out in the end," she said with quiet firmness to both of the young people, although each took the words for their own.

Kate nodded silently.

But Craig slammed a clenched fist down on the windowsill and cursed. "Damn! Damn it all! Why does it have to be this way? Why couldn't he just say, 'It's good to see you, boy,' or hold out a hand? I'd have walked across the room—across the continent—to take it." He had turned as he spoke, and his pain was etched on his face.

Arie stepped quickly to his side and laid a hand on his arm. Kate ached to do so.

"It will just take a little time, as Arie said," she ventured from across the room.

Craig turned dark, haunted eyes on her, but they lightened with surprise. "Kate! I forgot, I didn't see you."

"What?" It was Arie's turn to be surprised. "You mean you two are already acquainted?"

"Yes," Craig answered softly, a hint of a grin tugging at his lips. He gave no explanation.

"Yes, Arie," Kate echoed. "You see . . . well, remember that salesman I mentioned yesterday?"

"Oh, yes, I had the strangest feeling it was you, Craig, but couldn't let myself believe it." Arie turned a slightly puzzled glance from one to the other, then shrugged lightly. "More complications! Well, Kate, I'm going to be bold then and suggest you accompany Craig down the street for a bite of lunch. I had prepared a salad for us all . . . but I don't think—"

"That's a wonderful idea!" Kate nodded, eager to bring an end to the tension. She peeled off her smock, slipped a hand through Craig's arm, and headed for the door. "Arie, will you?"

"You two go on now. Don't worry. I'll take care of Will."

The wind had shifted, and a sharp breeze was blowing down off the mountains. It caught Kate's hair and tossed it about her face as she stepped out the front door. Craig stopped short and drew a deep, ragged breath. Kate turned her eyes away from his strained face, feeling she had no right. But his soft voice drew her gaze back.

"Sorry you had to see all that."

"Oh, don't be sorry, Craig, please. I only wish there were something I could do."

"This is *not* your fight, Kate."

"But I don't want it to be anyone's fight," she insisted, once again slipping her arm through his. She needed that warm, live touch of contact—and Craig looked like he could use it, too. "I want everyone to live happily ever after—"

Craig's hearty laugh turned the heads of the nearest passersby. "That's in fairy tales, Kate. I thought you were the practical one."

"Practical, yes." She sent her dark hair flying with a quick toss of her head. "But an incurable romantic deep in my innermost heart—" With a blush she added quickly, "And a starving one at that! Come on."

They walked close together down the windy

street. Kate pulled her collar closer about her throat, and Craig strode along with his hands thrust deep in his pockets. He was silent for a while, and Kate left him to his thoughts. Then he began to reminisce aloud. "Do you see that drugstore on the corner? I used to stop there for chocolate malts every day on the way home from school. And Ed Rangley's Hardware? He sponsored our Little League team, and his kid always got to be pitcher. And look over there, that bookstore there? That used to be Shroeder's Pack and Feed. I ran deliveries for old man Shroeder when I wasn't down helping in the clinic."

Craig was so caught up in his musings, he'd failed to notice the stir his own presence was causing. But Kate was suddenly very aware of the ripples of excitement in the street and shopfronts around them. One after another head turned, popped out a window, poked out a door. The rockers in front of the old market all ceased their rocking as the couple drew near. Finally one white-haired fellow pointed and called out in a shrill, excited voice: "Hey! Hey, you. Is that Craig Turner? Old Doc Turner's boy?"

Craig's eyes snapped into focus in the present. "Sure is." He grinned, then mounted the two steps to the market porch, his hand outstretched. "Well, hello, Mr. Crites. You're looking fit as a fiddle. Hello, Mr. Adams, Mr. Burchard." He shook hands all around, smiling but avoiding their questions with determined cheerfulness. "Excuse us now, the doctor here is taking me to lunch. Mustn't keep a lady waiting." And with a wink he was off the porch, slipped an arm around Kate's waist, and headed for the café.

One final obstruction lay in their path. Myrtle Kaiser, the town's self-appointed gossip columnist, 69-year-old philanthropic organizer and chairperson of *every* committee the Women's Club deemed worthy of coordinating. Craig groaned as she quickly crossed the street, her bottle-black hair bobbing, to encounter them head-on.

"Craig Turner! I do declare!" Her voice was high-pitched and carried like a kite caught on the wind. "My, my! What a treat to have you back in town! When did you get here? I hadn't heard a word about it!"

"Morning, Miss Kaiser. Pleasure to see you, too. You're looking as gorgeous as ever."

Kate watched the scene with detached amusement, admiring Craig's deference to the older woman as she planted herself in his path barring him from further movement. "You know, Craig, it's time for the annual hospital drive again." Her voice crooned on, and Kate winced at the woman's audacity in throwing Craig a pitch for one of her many fund raising drives. "And we simply can't do it without you, dear boy. Why"—she lowered her voice surreptitiously, believing Kate could not hear a word she was saying—"do you realize, Craig, dear, how many people you've helped with your donation to that east wing!"

Kate's brows shot up. She *had* heard—and could not believe her ears. The east wing was a five-year-old addition to the town's only hospital that contained all the latest equipment and made it possible for Hickory Ridge residents to have the laboratory work done locally rather than traveling the sixty miles to Roanoke. The funds had been donated anonymously, Will had told her, and no one seemed to have a clue as to the benefactor.

"Miss Kaiser, we have an agreement—" Craig's voice had an edge to it now. He glanced uneasily at Kate.

"Yes, yes, I know! People may think I tell all, but my lips are sealed!"

Craig's frown softened into a smile. "Why, Miss Kaiser, there's no one I'd rather trust with a secret." There was a teasing glimmer in his eyes that brought a scarlet blush to the spinster's dry cheeks. "Here." He pulled a business card out of his wallet and the figure of a golden horse flashed before Kate's eyes as he put the card in Myrtle's plump, eager fingers. "Call Jim Stanford at this number and he'll help you out. I'll let him know you'll be calling—"

"Oh, Craig, thank you," the woman gushed. "You're such a dear man . . . even if I'm the only one in this town who'll say so!" She hugged Craig impulsively, nodded grandiosely at Kate, and waddled on down the street.

"Snippity-bíbbet," Craig mumbled under his breath.

"What?"

"Snippity-bibbet. That's what my dad used to call Myrtle. I'd almost forgotten. Actually she's only that way with him because he gives her such a hard time. She's not a bad gal, if only she'd learn to corral that tongue now and then."

"Craig, what she said about the hospital . . ." She looked up at him with unveiled curiosity, her mouth open wide.

Craig looked down, then tapped her chin teasingly with one blunt fingertip. "I never gossip on an empty stomach, dear. Come on, I'm starving!" And before Kate could pursue the scene she had just witnessed, Craig had ushered her across the street and into the warm, sweet-smelling interior of the café.

It was a long rectangular room with a formica countertop and a row of backless stools at one end, and six sets of dinette tables and chairs at the other. There were no tablecloths on the tables, just red-and-white-checked napkins. But the little place gleamed, and behind the glass-fronted shelves lining the wall from kitchen door to front window was a dazzling array of home-baked pies and pastries.

Kate's mouth watered at the delicious mingling of aromas. "Yum-m-m. This is just what I need to recover from a great shock to my nervous system." Her heels tapped reproachfully across the linoleum floor, and she slid into one of the chairs. "Why do I keep getting the feeling when I'm with you that I've somehow stepped into the twilight zone?" She laughed, looking into his eyes as he took the seat across from her. "Honestly, I never know what to expect next. Even a walk down my own street is full of surprises."

"Don't you like surprises, Kate?" He covered her

hand with his, sending tiny shock waves of pleasure up her arm.

"Certainly," she answered, "but every minute? Of every day? I like my life simple, down to earth . . ."

"And I'm just a simple, down-to-earth guy—"

"I don't know *who* you are, but simple doesn't seem to fit the bill."

"Depends on what you mean by simple, I guess." Craig's voice drifted off, and Kate knew he didn't want to pursue the conversation. But she knew just as surely she couldn't let it drop.

"Craig, what *did* happen between you and your father? What could possibly have alienated you two so terribly?" She spread her hands in a gentle, apologetic gesture. "I'm sorry if it sounds like I'm prying. I don't mean to. But perhaps if I knew, I could help."

Craig looked at her steadily. Carefully. "That's nice, Kate. And I could use nice right now." He filled his lungs with a deep breath. "Okay, let's see. Maybe I can explain some of it. There isn't anything you can do to help, but at least you might understand me a little better." Craig stared into Kate's lovely green eyes and paused. Damn. He *did* want her to understand him. But why? He had never cared a tinker's damn about being understood by a woman before. Liked it much better when they didn't, in fact. And of all women, a veterinarian—and his father's partner, to boot! But her eyes were so wide and gentle. Like fern-green pools resting in the hollows of the hills, reflecting sunlight and storm. Accepting all. And her lashes were a dusky fringe sweeping down to brush her cheek as she blinked, watching him. Craig wanted her to like very much what she saw. So, fighting an unfamiliar tightness in his throat, he began to speak softly. "Do you know what I got for a college graduation present? No guesses? Well, it was a set of papers and the deed to some land. The papers were a completed application to Virginia State. My courses were chosen. My schedule confirmed. Vet school was just a step away. All it needed was my signature. And the funny thing was, I had thought of becoming a veterinarian. Hell, how could I have helped but, with it being hammered into my head for a solid eighteen years." He clenched a fist on the table in front of him, then slowly uncurled the fingers, straining to hold back the tension. "I had thought of following in my father's footsteps, pacing myself to his stride. But . . ." His smoldering eyes were focused somewhere in the space between them. "I was just aching to step out on my own. I could feel it like a fire in my body." His lids slid down, hiding his eyes. His hand opened and closed and opened again. "But I signed the papers. I went off to school. I lasted two years."

"And then?" she prompted into the silence.

"Well, the irony of the whole damn thing is that I love animals—not in the all-consuming way my father does, but in my own way. I've always wanted to work with horses. So I did . . . do. Bought myself a place up north a ways"—he laughed harshly—"and lived happily ever after."

"But Craig, surely your father could understand

67

that, especially after all these years, all the water under the bridge—"

"Nope! It never flowed under the bridge, Kate. Just got all dammed up. There were other complications. Remember the deed I mentioned? Well, I sold the land he had given me. Used it for a downpayment on my own place."

"The graduation present?" Kate's voice sounded small even to her own ears.

"The graduation present. Inheritance. Empire. Heritage. It doesn't matter what you call it—even blackmail. The point is, it had been Turner land and I sold it." Challenge and regret and despair were all mixed in his tone, mirrored in his handsome face.

Kate waited a moment, her eyes fastened on the flat, stained surface of the table. Then she looked at him again. When she spoke, her voice trembled with emotion.

"You must have known how your father would feel, Craig. To him land is life—"

"Don't lecture me!" His lips were white-edged, his eyes narrowed. "Of course I knew. But I was twenty years old!" His tongue flicked over dry lips. "It bought me *my* life."

"At what price?" She willed the words back even as she voiced them.

"It's *my* price. And I'm paying it."

Kate caught her bottom lip between her teeth and sat still as she spoke. Her heart ached.

There was silence.

"I'm sorry," she said at last.

"So am I. About a lot of things."

"Craig, wasn't there any other way? Some way he could understand? A compromise?" Her soft voice lifted with hope. "He's really such a good man, your father."

"Is he? And what about me?" Craig's stormy, dark eyes held her. "No, Kate. There was no way I could see. Not then. Not at twenty. He wouldn't listen to me. Wouldn't hear what I was saying, I had my own dreams to live."

He set the words on the table between them like a bowl or a piece of fruit. They were there. He wasn't asking for sympathy or condemnation. And he had left himself open to both. She saw it in his eyes. It made her heart stop. That stubborn pride tinged with regret disarmed her. Melted her into tenderness.

"Oh, Craig. But later—couldn't you talk to him all these years?"

"Talk to the old man? You really *don't* know him. Give him a sick cow and he'll wear himself out worrying over it. But a rebellious son? Never!"

"You tried?"

"Of course I tried!" His voice stung like a whip. "Sorry, Kate. Yes, I tried. But my father is a bitter, unforgiving man. He hates me. He drove me away." Craig's eyes blazed blue fire. Muscles moved along his jaw.

Again, Kate lowered her eyes, his anguish was so fierce.

She barely heard his whisper. "My mother died

69

while I was gone. I came back for the funeral and never again."

"Craig . . ." Kate's voice was a choked whisper. "I'm so sorry."

"So am I. I know she missed me. The fight hurt her, although she was too loyal to ever say anything against Dad. Then it was too late."

"But now you're back! And you're going to try again—"

"Closing the barn door after the cows got out."

"Better than nothing. And I'll help."

"Oh, no, you don't. I told you, this is not your fight." Despite his retort, a smile had flickered across the gloom on his face. It lingered at the corners of his mouth. "Kate, you can help by ordering lunch and dropping the whole subject. Waitress—"

"But, Craig—"

"No, Kate!"

"Hey! Remember who you are talking to—the eternal romantic."

"And they lived happily ever after?"

"You bet!"

"Hello, dearies. Sorry to keep you waiting." A pink, plump hand waved two menus in the air before their faces. The hand belonged to an equally pink, plump waitress who had materialized out of thin air at their table side on rubber-soled shoes. "Sorry to keep you. Ready to order now?"

"Kate?"

"I'll have a BLT and a Coke, please, with a side order of fries and a bowl of succotash."

Craig groaned. "I'll have the same, minus the extras. And a chocolate malt—for old times' sake."

Echoing the order in rather strident tones, the waitress disappeared through the kitchen door.

Kate had watched her noisy exit, and Craig sat watching Kate. He felt suddenly peaceful and easy, as if he had waded into a cool mountain brook. Calmed. Refreshed. His eyes drank the coolness of her skin. Savored the tilt of her chin, the curve of her cheek, the shadow of those long, dark lashes. Never had he spoken aloud the words he had just spilled across the table. They had been eating at his insides for years, a constant, gnawing pain. But if Kate Harrington could hear those words and still smile that lovely smile at him, then perhaps there was hope. Hell, a man could pin his hopes on a bit of blue sky— or the sea-green eyes of a beautiful woman. It felt a lot better than despair.

Craig rolled his shoulders inside the loose fit of his sweater. And Kate could almost see the tension draining from him.

From him and into her, as he reached across the table and stroked his fingers down her arm. "We have shared some interesting levels of intimacy in a brief twenty-four hours, Dr. Harrington."

A quiver ran through her. "Of that, Mr. Turner, I am well aware. What have you done to my calm, pleasant life?"

He grinned. "You tell me."

But she wouldn't, couldn't. Instead she laughingly

drew her arm away, her hand slipping finally from the warmth of his touch.

"Lunchtime!"

They sat for a while after and talked lightly of things, then stepped back out onto the street and into the bright splash of fall sunshine.

"Hm-m-m! I knew it was going to be a gorgeous day," Kate breathed, flinging her arms wide open and drinking in a long, refreshing breath.

She never got to release that breath.

Craig slid his arms around her body, scooped her up to his chest, and bent his tawny head over her dark one. Street and stores fell away. The deep blueness of the autumn sky tilted around them, descending in swift silence like a bell jar, or they, like swimmers sinking in a bubble to the bottom of the sea. Far down in the sensitive, betraying depths of her body there rose a hidden spring of passion. It washed through her, rising and warmly spreading through her limbs. His lips came closer and closer, lowering over hers, their breath merging before their lips ever touched. His fragrance filled her head, heightened her senses—that musky blend of aftershave, warm skin, and desire. His fingers tightened at her back; and at his touch, instinctively, like a stroked cat, she arched and curved against the waiting heat of his flesh.

And then his mouth came down hard on hers, his lips warm and moist, sweet and demanding. His lips opened, and then her own opened in undeniable response. The gentle but urgent probing of his

72

tongue as it slipped between her yielding lips and into the secret, delicious cave of her mouth. Her newly awakened passion swept through her like a flood and left her skin fragile and flushed. She was aware at every point of contact of his controlled and subtle power—his thighs against her thighs, his hips pressed against hers, his chest and shoulders and hands. And always his mouth, his mouth searching and finding, draining her kisses and will. Her head spinning. Her heart pounding. Her pulse fluttering at wrist and temple.

Then he released her. The street firmed beneath her feet; the sky ascended. Against her will the world swam back into focus.

And Craig stood above her, smiling. "I just wanted to thank you for . . . for listening." And then more softly, " 'Bye for now."

And he was gone.

Kate stood there, one hand pressed to her throat as she struggled to put the world back in its place. "A box of candy would have been fine," she murmured to his departing back.

Then she turned back toward the clinic. And only then realized that half the town had been privy to their first kiss.

CHAPTER THREE

Kate sat on the smooth wooden step outside the cabin door and pulled the collar of her sweater up around her throat. The wind whistled gently through the trees, tugging at the golden leaves that obligingly released their grasp and fell into bronze patches upon the ground. A slight frown marred her brow, but every now and again the shadow of a smile played across her lips. Inwardly, her emotions were playing that same game of tug-of-war; and she was the rope beginning to fray.

That man had kissed her—in the middle of Main Street! Oh, it made her furious just to think of it. How could she have let that happen? But how exciting that it had. Her lips remembered the touch of his: her body still felt his heat.

Fiddlesticks, woman. Don't make more out of this

than there is. For all you know, you may never see him again. The corner of her mouth quirked upward. Well, she thought, her lips pursed in a sensuous pout, see him, yes. But kiss him? Hickory Ridge is not likely to witness a sequel to that famous first act. Unh-unh! With a toss of her dark head, she climbed noisily up the steps, let the door swing to with a hearty slam, and set about making dinner.

All through her meal, and the quiet evening beyond, she muttered and argued at Ginger, assuring the big golden dog and herself that Mr. Craig Turner wasn't worth another minute's thought. Her dreams proved to be rebels, opening the door for his presence as for a welcome, long-awaited guest. Kate woke up thinking about him. Drove to work thinking about him.

One look at Will's set face and Aunt Arie's deeply etched worry lines told Kate that Craig was on everyone's mind this morning.

"What's on the calendar today, Dr. Turner?" she asked, slipping into her white smock.

"Not a doggone thing worth messin' with," came the burly reply.

That meant small-animal work, Kate knew. "To hear you talk, you'd think you hated any creature under the size of a moose, Will! But I've seen through you, Doc. Saw you petting Mac's new red-bone pup . . ."

Will's dour look cut her short. "Wound up tighter than a clock this morning, aren't you, Dr. Harrington? Bad enough I've got a day filled with cats and pups and someone's leftover Easter bunny. Don't need to talk about 'em, do I?"

He harrumphed and grumbled his way through the first three visits. Arie and Kate exchanged knowing glances, but neither had the courage, nor the heart, to broach the subject or mention Craig's name.

At lunchtime, Arie called them into the dining room. The table was set for four. Will took one look, turned, and stalked off to his garden. He began snipping at things. Snipping off roses and magnolia branches and half-grown marigolds. Then he started on the bushes that lined the north edge of the yard and trimmed them until the rough brown branches poked through.

Kate watched him for a good five minutes, then turned. She was amazed to see Arie already seated, chewing steadily on a biscuit.

"Aunt Arie, what's going to happen?"

"You and I are going to eat lunch, child. Other than that, who knows?"

"But the extra chair—? Were you expecting Craig?"

"I was hoping. One of them is going to have to make the first move. I was hoping it would be Craig. He knows his father's routine, knew he'd be here now."

"What about yesterday? Doesn't Craig's coming home count as a first move, a peace overture?"

"Nope. That was just the gathering of the armies. They haven't brought in the big guns yet."

76

"Oh, Arie. Do you mean it's going to be a real knock-down, drag-out fight?"

Arie put her half-eaten biscuit back on the plate and touched her napkin to her lips. "Have you ever known two stubborn, hardheaded men to do anything but?"

"Can't we help? Craig told me about their fight. How it started—" Kate let her words drift off, hoping for some encouragement.

"Knowing about it doesn't make it yours, Kate. Don't break your heart over it."

"But—"

"But what, Katherine?" the old woman asked softly.

"But you know how much I care for Will and . . ."

"And?" Arie's steady, pained eyes held the younger woman's, pulling the reluctant words from her lips.

"And Craig seems to be a nice man, a good man," Kate answered, blushing.

"Very nice, Kate. And good, certainly. I don't know of any finer. But he's stubborn as the day is long."

"Then they need our help!"

Arie smiled. "And they're going to get it whether they want it or not. Right, child? I can see the fire sparking in those green eyes!"

"Well, Arie," Kate grinned fondly at the older woman, "you haven't seen anything yet."

Kate's fire had dimmed during the long, silent afternoon. Evening found her back on the cabin steps.

"Darn it all!" she muttered, staring off at the gilt-edged peaks. What was happening to the promise of these mountains—the peace and quiet and desperately craved equilibrium that had brought her into their midst? To cool, levelheaded Kate, the effect of this handsome, irreverent stranger made no sense at all. Yet all her efforts to forget the rapturous touch of his hard, lean body against hers, to disavow the strange euphoric feeling that filled her when she thought of those laughing eyes, were to no avail. Oh, Kate! she scolded herself as she lightly fingered a leaf near her foot. Stop! It's just a slight case of culture shock, that's all. After all, it had been a long time since she had been touched by a man—and whatever else he might be, Craig Turner was most definitely a man!

At that moment Ginger came bounding around the corner of the cabin and came to a sliding stop alongside her master. The furry animal licked Kate's hand in long, wet laps, then looked up into her face with soulful eyes. Kate laughed. "All right, Ginger. You win! Let's walk. She rose to her feet in one fluid movement and with Ginger at her heels, headed up the mountain path that ran alongside the narrow access road. The breeze caught her hair and it floated like a black mane behind her as she and Ginger sprinted up the mountain slope. At last Kate stopped, her breath coming in labored spurts. "Have mercy, my friend. I am not nearly as adept on these slopes as you are!" Ginger acquiesced and soon the two were moving along the path at a more comfortable gait.

The sun had sunk to the hem of the pines along the west ridge now, and cast long shadows across the path. Golden, rosy hues of sunlight sliced through the trees and lit their way. Ginger and Kate stood in the hush of the mountainside enjoying the sunset. For a moment all they heard was the soft movement of the breeze through the trees. Then Ginger's ears perked up. As Kate's senses became attuned to her surroundings, she heard it, too. A soft, almost primitive sound, floating down over the treetops, curling about the woman and her dog like a magical spell. The sweet, gentle strains of music sifted down through the twisted tree branches and drew the hikers forward along the path. As they neared a clearing, the music became more pronounced and Kate recognized the clear, melodic notes of a stringed instrument. She moved forward, unafraid, finding an unexplainable security in the beauty of the music ahead. As she emerged into the clearing, a strange sight greeted her eyes. A small, rough log cabin edged the clearing on one side, backed by a thick cluster of trees and surrounded by an assortment of woodpiles, barrels, carving tools, and other less definable objects. Across the clearing from where Kate stood was a small camp fire, and beside it sat two blue-jeaned men, one strumming gently and delicately on an oval-shaped instrument. As Kate drew closer, one of the men turned toward her footsteps.

"My beautiful Kate . . ." Craig Turner tried in vain to rise to his feet.

Immediately Kate felt a flash of response to his

voice—a gentle swimming sensation in her limbs and a fluid warmth that washed over her. Even now, as she met his slightly inebriated gaze.

"Kate . . . Kate, so good of you to come. . . ." His words drifted off into an indecipherable collection of syllables, and Kate recognized on his face the dazed expression from sour-mash whiskey. She tore her eyes away and focused her attention on the young, bearded man sitting beside Craig. He gazed up at Kate with a warm, slightly blurred, look of welcome, reserved in these parts for greeting old friends.

"Ah, you must be Doctor Kate." He stretched out one hand and beckoned her closer. "Come, share our fire . . . guaranteed to burn more brightly with such a beautiful woman at its side."

A giggle began to build in Kate's throat as she watched the two grown men, their faces awash in boyish innocence, their empty bottles strewn about the clearing. In seconds she was laughing out loud, low and heartily . . . and unable to stop. She brushed the glistening tears away with the back of her hand and slid down on the wide log beside Craig, her chest still pulsating with mirth. Ginger, having satisfied herself that the situation was safe, planted her furry body comfortably between Craig's heavy boots. Craig laid a hand on Kate's knee. Immediately she felt the outline of each finger on her smooth skin and the flash of electricity that shot through her limbs. "Kate . . ." Craig sought her eyes as a slow, crooked smile played on his lips. "Kate, calm your-shelf . . . whatever is my friend here going to think of you?" His eyes caressed her face in playfulness, and Kate sat up straight, seeking in the movement some distance between his thigh and her own.

Jeremy watched the two solemnly, then looked at Kate alone, his face breaking into a wide grin encased in an unruly, red-tinged beard. "Kate . . . truly . . . a pleasure to meet you. I've heard many wonderful things about you. I'm Jeremy McFadden, and welcome to my humble home. . . ." His hand swept the cluttered clearing.

"Thank you, Jeremy"—again, laughter filled her and she struggled with her words—"and it is indeed a pleasure to meet you. What . . . what do you do up here?" Her laughing eyes shifted to the large wooden barrels bordering the cabin, then came to rest on the wooden instrument in Jeremy's lap. "Why . . . why what a beautiful dulcimer!" The long, oval-shaped instrument was beautifully carved with strips of dark wood inlaid into its smooth surface, their polished lines forming a small unicorn.

Jeremy beamed with pleasure. He leaned over and set it in Kate's lap for her closer scrutiny. "Careful, it's magic, you know . . . like the Pied-Piper."

She laughed again as she ran her fingers over the beautifully crafted instrument. "Well, it did lure Ginger and me up here, I guess. Did you make this, Jeremy?"

He nodded modestly, then took the dulcimer back and began playing soft chords on the taut strings. "That, lovely lady, is what I do." The mysterious strain quickly spun a web about them, and Kate became lost in its beauty. For a moment she was in a faraway world, floating on the cushion of beautiful music, surrounded by the fresh scent of pine trees and mountain flowers. She closed her eyes, wrapped her hands around her knees, and gave in to the heady blend of fantasy and the mountain setting. A heavy weight against her shoulder jarred her out of her reverie. Craig had slumped sideways until his body was blocked from falling by her own. His head leaned forward until it rested against her, nuzzling into the graceful curve of her neck and shoulder. His eyes were closed, and a peaceful smile lined his rugged face.

Kate shuddered, suddenly aware of his unshaven skin against her own. A faint, disturbingly masculine odor floated about her, and she shifted on the log. Craig's eyelids fluttered but remained closed to the outside world. Kate looked down where his hand still rested on her leg. Now she could feel the gentle pressure of his fingertips as they rested on the soft skin, bared by her worn walking shorts. His warm breath brushed against her neck and she felt her pulse quicken. The heightened sensations—his touch, his scent, his warmth—were all sharpened by the stillness of the approaching dusk, and Kate found herself wanting to draw him closer, to touch his face, his chest, to explore his body, to feel the smoothness of his lips upon her own.

Exhaling sharply, Kate pushed a space between them. Craig's head lolled, then jerked upright. A slow, crooked smile spread across his face. "Good morning, Kate . . ."

Kate glanced over at Jeremy, her eyes seeking help. "How long has Craig been up here, Jeremy?" The breeze had shifted as the sun slipped down the side of the mountain, and washed them in coolness.

Jeremy's eyes focused, and his voice was clear of the earlier fogginess when he replied, "Since last night. We've been friends forever, and he needed a friend to lean on for a while. Unfortunately"—his eyes grinned as they settled on his friend—"Craig's not much of a drinker. I'm afraid my home brew made him lean a little too much. Which seems to leave us with a bit of a problem. He's been camping out up here, but it's supposed to get pretty cold tonight."

Kate looked hopefully at the roughly put together log house. "What about your cabin?"

"Built for one, unfortunately. You see, I don't get a lot of overnight guests up here." Jeremy pushed himself to a standing position, and for the first time, Kate noticed the hand-carved crutches at his side. Her eyes were drawn to the strong leg upon which he stood, then to the other pants leg that narrowed at the knee, then curved around a smooth post to the ground. Jeremy followed her glance. "Oh. You hadn't noticed my peg leg? Lost it in Nam. Hey . . ." He immediately responded to Kate's look. "I'm fine out here. As long as we don't have an infestation of termites!" His laugh was infectious and immediately dispelled the moment of awkwardness. "But," Jeremy

83

continued, "I'm not really up to caring for Craig tonight. Besides the fact that he eats too damn much! Don't suppose you could take him down to your place?"

Kate's brows lifted, and she shot a glance at Craig. He was still on the log next to her, half-listening, his head nodding at regular intervals.

"He's an honorable guy, Kate. I'll swear to it! Isn't a better man to be found."

"Oh, I'm sure he's honorable, Jeremy." There was an edge to her voice, but her eyes lingered on Craig. She couldn't explain to Jeremy that it wasn't really Craig's restraint that worried her. Her emotions were playing such an irrational game of cat and mouse these past few days. How could she spend another night in her cabin with Craig Turner . . . and keep everything calm and cool and uncomplicated?

"Well," Kate spoke aloud, "I guess one more night wouldn't kill me. And he is Will's son. But *one* more. And that's it, Jeremy!"

"That's all he needs, Kate. One night. Honest. He'll have to make some decisions tomorrow—"

Kate's eyes were questioning, but Jeremy was silent.

"Well, Jeremy." Kate rose to her feet. "How do you propose that we handle the logistics of getting him down the mountain? Roll him?"

"Not a bad idea! But if we can pour him into his car over there"—Jeremy pointed to a small Chevette half-hidden in the trees, a rent-a-car sticker visible on the back window—"it might be faster—"

"All right, perhaps if Ginger pulls and you and I push." The two laughingly eyed the six-foot-three frame stretched out on the bench. Soon, with Craig's dazed cooperation, they managed to fold him into the passenger side of the small car. Kate brushed the twigs and debris off her shorts and ran a hand over her perspiring forehead. "Give me pigs in surgery any day," she moaned. "All right now, Jeremy, wish me luck—"

As Jeremy held the door open, she slid in behind the wheel.

"Thanks, Kate. Now I owe you one. Come back and see me soon." Jeremy closed the door, waved, and made his way back to the cabin. Kate watched him disappear through the door, took a deep breath, and leaned forward to turn the keys. Her fingers slid over the smooth ignition switch. It was empty. She glanced up quickly, but Jeremy had disappeared from sight.

"Craig . . . Craig . . ." Kate gently shook the large frame next to her. "Craig, I need your keys." Craig's eyelids fluttered, then opened halfway and focused with a fleeting stab of sobriety. "Keys? Kate? In my pocket . . ." And immediately the heavy lids closed as his head leaned against the door in a peaceful slumber.

Kate felt the chest pocket in his shirt but, as she had feared, it was as smooth as glass "Oh, no—" She moaned as her eyes traveled down his body to the tight jeans hugging his hips. The clear outline of a key ring bulged at the precise angle where his hip met his thigh. Kate shook him again, but to no avail. Gingerly she slipped three fingers into the tight space between the two pieces of denim. She paused, then pushed farther, her fingers stretching toward their mark. She could feel the warmth of his skin through the worn material. Kate clenched her eyes tightly in a vain effort to dispel the hot, liquid feeling that surged through her body.

She glanced back at Ginger, who sat quietly on the backseat, her head cocked to one side, watching the drama being enacted before her with a curious, amused look on her golden face. "Ginger, don't you dare repeat a word of this to anyone!"

Then her fingers made one final plunge toward the missing keys, bringing immediate life to the previously limp form. A sensuous gasp escaped his lips as Kate's face burned with the hot flush that seared it, coating her ears and throat. She jerked her hand out, the keys dangling from one bent finger. "Craig, I'm sorry, but—"

"Sorry? Don't be." His dazed eyes glinted with humor and pleasure. "Keep up the good work!"

Kate jabbed the keys into the ignition and gunned the engine as she fought to calm the tide of emotion rising within her. "Go back to sleep!" she commanded, and his lids once again closed obediently as Craig's husky laugh drifted out the open window.

Later, she wouldn't be able to remember how she and Ginger had managed to get Craig Turner—all two hundred solid pounds of him—into the cabin. But manage they somehow did, and soon, Kate, with Craig balanced precariously at her side, stood in the center of the large bedroom. She paused for a moment, enjoying the warmth of his body against her own, feeling the pulse of life within him. As her eyes moved to his face, she jerked back, releasing her hold and letting her arms fall quickly to her side. Craig's eyes were open, encompassing her, and a smile of obvious enjoyment played at the corners of his mouth. He leaned abruptly to one side as his main support put a fast two feet between them. Craig took a step toward her, but Kate jerked her hands up, planting them firmly against his broad chest. "Oh, no, you don't! I'm warning you, Craig Turner—you back off now. . . ."

Craig grinned, then took a cautious step backward. "Yes, ma'am. Is this far enough?" His head began to bob as his eyes fought to hold her in focus.

Kate looked at him and raised one brow. "Well, I was thinking more of Portland." With renewed determination she guided him onto the bed, tugged off his mud-caked boots, and eased the sluggish form down onto the pillows. She quickly unbuttoned his shirt, slipped his arms out of it, and draped it over a chair. Her fingers rested on his belt buckle, then quickly dropped off as if seared by a hidden fire.

"No," she whispered. "That's one job I definitely can't handle tonight." She pulled a light sheet up over the still body and said softly, "Well, Mr. Turner, this is the last time . . . the very last time . . .

you're sleeping in my . . . er . . . our house—so enjoy it." But her words were blocked by the sealing of his lids and the tight blanket of sleep wrapped about him. Kate smiled at the suddenly vulnerable form, then turned, quietly flicked the light switch, and slipped out of the room.

Kate stirred beneath the covers, oblivious of the passing hours. Her fingers curled into a loose fist and she rolled over onto her side. The warmth of her body had combined with the warmth of her blanket to create a snug, toasty little nest. Her body lay loose and open in the soft heat, and there was a slight flush on her cheeks. Only the pillow was cool—cool now beneath her cheek as her hair spilled loose to the side, fanning dark smoke against the white pillow-case.

But again something disturbed her, reaching down into the floating depths of her sleep. Calling her up . . . up . . . up to the surface.

Her lips parted and she murmured, a sleepy half-syllable without meaning. The warmth held her, but something was drawing her up . . . up. . . . Her eyelids fluttered. She drew a deeper breath, pulling the cool night air of the cabin into her being. The breath carried something at its heart: a scent, almost a familiar taste. She turned again beneath the covers, one arm lifting and stretching out of the warmth, falling heavily across the covers; one bare arm, the pale silky skin tightening into goose bumps in the chill air. And she stirred, and opened her eyes, and came awake.

And open, vulnerable as she was, fresh from sleep, every sense immediately registered his presence.

Craig sat at the foot of her bed. Watching her. His eyes were hidden by the shadows so that she could not read them. But his gaze was like a physical touch upon her body. Stroking her. Caressing her. Softly. Without threat. With more like wonder.

"Hello, Kate. I woke you. I'm sorry."

"It's all right, Craig," she replied sleepily. And then, "Are you all right?"

"Yes. Now." A low, self-conscious laugh. "I think I had a few too many sips of Jeremy's moonshine."

"I'd say you had at least your share," Kate teased, glad to keep the talk neutral, away from herself, or his half-naked presence at the foot of her bed.

For now she was seeing him more clearly, with the sleep and surprise lifting from her eyes. He was wearing only his jeans, as she had left him. But he must have just showered, for the wetness still clung to his hair, and a sprinkling of it lay across his shoulders. It caught and held her eyes like the sparkle of a hypnotist's crystal. She saw his torso, bare and dark and gleaming where the wetness clung. The wide span of his shoulders merged into shadow. He appeared more massive than she had remembered, his muscles beautifully defined beneath his bare skin. But his hair was a light, tousled mane that caught and held the dim light.

Looking at him, Kate wasn't afraid, but her heart

was fluttering wildly in her breast, her breath caught in her suddenly tight throat. It was becoming an all-too-familiar response. But she mustn't let him see—or guess.

"You were quite a sight when I happened upon you two up at Jeremy's place," she said lightly.

"I bet!" Again his laughter rumbled in his chest. "But you, Kate . . . you were a dream, conjured up by the firelight, the flames shining in your hair and eyes. Actually I thought I *was* dreaming . . . until I woke up here—"

"Craig," she whispered warningly. "I—"

"Don't be afraid. It's all right, Kate." She could see the flash of his smile. "I hope I didn't say or do anything out of line?"

"No." She smiled back, shaking her head, and her hair rippled like ebony seawaves across the pillow. "No. You were a perfect—if unconscious—gentleman."

"Well, then perhaps I could try again. Now."

He leaned across her, his weight settling heavily on top of her. She could feel the hard, lean length of him: legs, thighs, hips, chest, shoulders. His breath was on her neck, stirring her hair where it clung to her suddenly damp skin. All of her felt damp. Wet, heavy, and immobilized with desire. The old flame, shooting and leaping up her loins, centered deep within her—that old flame she had quenched and replaced with cool rationality. Now reason evaporated in the heat of her passion, and the old flame . . . But no, no, not the same, not that bright, early

90

fire of inexperienced excitement. . . . What *he* had awakened in her the other afternoon with his kiss, and what she felt tonight with his weight upon her, his breath in her hair, was a darker, fiercer burning. A lick of fire along her spine. Its bright feathers of flame traveling and jumping along her nerves, from womb to fingertips, from the top of her skull to tiptoe.

"Oh, Craig . . ." Afraid to say yes, unable to say no, she bit her lips to stifle her words.

"Katherine . . ." He whispered her name in a way no man had ever said it before. "Katherine, if I'm still dreaming, don't wake me. Just hold me. Hold me."

He turned his face as he spoke, whispering the words against the warm, flushed skin of her cheek, murmuring still as his lips brushed across her mouth. His lips were warm and firm against her mouth, brushing back and forth across her tight-pressed lips until they parted and opened almost of their own accord. Kate moaned. Her lips were suddenly eager to return his kisses. She yielded to the firm pressure of his mouth. He turned his face over hers, dusting kisses over her nose and eyelids, her cheeks and the corners of her mouth. "Katherine . . ."

Then his kiss deepened. She could feel his hunger take him. Heard the ragged edge of his breath. The tips of their tongues touched, and Kate shivered. The thrill of it made her pulse race. He was delicious. The velvety smoothness of his mouth, the polished hardness of his teeth, the clean slightly mint taste on his lips.

Kate fought her own desire. Tightened and drew away. Raising herself shakily onto one elbow, she leaned over him, looking at him with her fierce, leaf-green eyes. Her eyes had all the depth and mystery, the untouchability of the forests.

"No."

She saw his eyes go dark, quite dark, the pupils dilating. Beads of sweat from passion dotted his upper lip. Slowly she drew her fingertip across his damp mouth. "You are something else, Craig Turner."

"So are you, babe. I told you that first night. You're a spellbinder, and I'm trapped in your magic." He nipped the sensitive pad of her fingertip between his strong, white teeth.

Kate drew her hand away. "Mine is a slow magic, Craig. Slow and careful. Yours is too fast for me."

Husky laughter curled from his throat. "Why wait, when everything's so perfect right now?" His dark, narrowed eyes glinted with desire. Curving one bare arm around her shoulder, he stroked the back of her neck beneath the fall of her hair. "Why wait?"

"Because I want to. And because I like to make some of the decisions, too. All right?" Her full, kiss-swollen mouth tilted in a smile. She bent and brushed his lips with her own. "But you *are* something else!"

Craig crossed his arms behind his head and dropped back onto the soft feather pillows. His eyes caressed her face. "I can wait, Kate. Don't want to—but I can. So, boss, what do we do now?"

"*We* go back to our own beds, and go to sleep. Do

you hear those birds? That hush of wind in the trees? That's the whisper of the hills, telling us it'll soon be morning. So for tonight we go back to sleep . . . and tomorrow we'll see about tomorrow."

CHAPTER FOUR

Kate stood in the doorway to the second bedroom, still as a mouse in the dawn light. She was watching Craig sleep. His mouth was curved in a dreamlike smile. His sandy-colored hair fell softly across his forehead. She saw the quick dream-movement of his eyes beneath his lowered lids as one bare arm flung loose the quilt, revealing a tanned slice of his chest and belly.

Kate stepped closer, and as she watched him she experienced a resurgence of the fierce joy she had felt when their bodies touched and their lips met. It was accompanied by the flash of a desire to jump right into bed with him. The decision would certainly be hers! Grinning, she wrapped her hands around her elbows, gave him one last lingering look, and left.

Craig sighed softly. For just a moment there he had thought she was going to slip down beside him into this warm nest. He was ready—not to mention willing and able. This woman had him lit up like fireworks on the Fourth of July. He adored the way her green eyes laughed and sparked. He was bewitched by the curve of her cheek in the shadows of that raven-dark hair. Even the way she said no. Damn! If rejection felt that good, a yes would probably turn him inside out! Ummm . . . One lid snapped open and he peeked as far into the hallway as he could. "Come on back, babe," he whispered.

He heard the front door click open and shut, and with a shrug of his broad shoulders and a look of infinite patience, he settled back into the warm quilts.

The early morning air was tinged with an autumn chill that tickled its way down Kate's jacket collar. Shivering, she slipped into the Land Rover, shifted into first, and headed for work.

As she entered the outskirts of town, she exchanged a wave and a smile with the officer whose two-toned police car was hidden behind the billboard advertising Hickory Ridge's homespun cordiality. He was waiting patiently, practiced hunter that he was, for the inevitable tourist speeding happily down these mountain roads. Kate steered her car into the parking lot in front of the clinic and brushed a hand across her suddenly determined forehead. *She* could talk to Will, could make him see how stubborn he was being; make him understand that blood ties run deep. And need nurturing and forgiveness.

"Morning, Arie!" Kate greeted the older woman with an affectionate peck on the cheek as she moved quickly into the office.

"Good morning, Kate." Arie's voice seemed tired today, Kate thought. But of course, she was concerned, too.

"Arie," Kate ventured, hesitantly. "I . . . I saw Craig last night."

"Craig?" Arie's brows shot up. "Then he's still here?"

"Yes," Kate answered, then went on to fill Arie in as briefly as she could on Craig's visit to Jeremy, carefully eliminating any reference to her own very hospitable role. "I don't know whether he's going to try to see Will again. I think perhaps he's planning on leaving for a while, but, Arie—it's such a damn shame!" There was more feeling in her voice than she had intended. "Why can't he and Will talk? Why can't they work this out like two adults? They're both acting like children! And they're . . . they're only hurting themselves—"

"Yes, dear"—Arie's eyes were soft and loving but hazed with a strange distance—"you're right. They are hurting themselves. But some wounds never heal."

"Mornin', ladies!" Will's gruff baritone sliced through the room, putting a halt to Arie's words.

96

"Well, why are you just sitting around like two hens waiting for the eggs to hatch? We've got work to do."

"Yes, Doctor!" Kate threw Arie a we'll-finish-this-later look and followed Will through the door to the surgery.

"Will," she said to his flannel-shirted back, "I'd like to talk—"

"Me, too, Katie, but that doesn't pay the bills nor heal the animals, does it now? So get your smock on and let's prepare for the day." His voice was firm, but Kate was sure she detected a softness that had been missing this last week, ever since Craig walked into the office.

With renewed determination and a spurt of boldness, she shoved the schedule pad into his hands and tapped it with one tapered index finger. "As you can see, Dr. Turner, our first patients don't arrive for thirty-five minutes. That gives us plenty of time to prepare—"

"Hrumph," Will snorted noncommittally, and handed the pad back. He sat down and shuffled some papers on his desk. His shoulders seemed more stooped, and the lines edging his mouth seemed deeper today. The skin along his jaw seemed slack and paper thin.

"Will . . ." Kate rubbed a hand lightly across his shoulders. "Will, do you feel all right?"

The old man paused, and then without looking up at Kate, he lifted one hand and placed it on top of hers. "I'm old, Kate. An old man. And that's how I feel. Old. Tired." He gave her hand a quick squeeze.

"But thank the Lord the body still works and will continue to—at least for a while." He smiled up at her. "And when it can't go anymore, that's okay, too. I'm due for a little rest. And now I have you to care for the land and the animals—"

"Just stop that now, Will! This is no way to start the morning. Besides, knowing you, you'll outlive us all—out of pure orneriness!" Kate laughed lightly, anxious to draw Will out of this fatalistic mood.

"No, Kate. It would be foolish to pretend, and I'm nobody's fool!" He cracked a wide smile. "Listen, gal, dying isn't anything new. I've known it was going to happen for quite a few decades now!" He laughed at his own joke, then continued, "But I've got an edge, Katie, because I've always known *where* I was going to die—here, on my own land, in the midst of my work. A man needs to know that, Kate . . . needs to have that information to give his life its proper quality and his work its proper conclusion."

His words and tone moved her deeply, and Kate felt compelled to voice the words she had withheld until now. "Craig needs to know that, too, Will."

The smile dropped from Will's face. He didn't lash out in anger as Kate expected but rose slowly to his feet and stood in the middle of the room, his gaze traveling out the sashed window to the fields beyond. "Craig needed to know that, but he never took the time to learn. Instead he destroyed it. Gave it away. A Judas . . . for his thirty pieces of silver."

The room grew cold but not from the gust of autumn breeze that slipped in the door as Will left.

The rest of the morning passed in outward harmony, but something sad and unspoken drifted between Will and Arie and Kate. The old man worked beside Kate efficiently but silently, his very silence forbidding her to resume their earlier conversation.

Kate felt horribly embarrassed. How had her loving nature caused her to overstep such an obvious boundary? And now the discomfort, the pain that was there between them all. Kate read stubbornly through pages of reports from the state veterinary board, saw to the assortment of small animals scheduled for that morning, punched the buttons on her phone with unwanted force as she dialed to confirm recommended treatments and check on progress. She obstinately concentrated on her work—or tried to.

Her thoughts were running wild again; out of control, they insisted on returning to the emotional turmoil at hand. Her musings dwelt on Will and Craig and her own confused position between the two. A kind of irrational sense of betrayal twisted itself into her feelings when she recalled the erotic pleasure Craig had awakened in her the night before. And now? Was Craig up? Eating breakfast? Was he wearing those low-slung, thigh-hugging jeans? Or was he walking naked, golden skin shining in the morning light, through the small, familiar rooms of her cabin. Was he thinking of her? Her heart fluttered in her breast, a tiny fragile bird doing dizzying spins within her skin. From beneath lowered lashes, she cast a quick glance at Will across the room, then ran a hand across the damp back of her neck. Oh, goodness, how she yearned to pull the uncomplicated peace of the hills about her again. If only she could turn the clock back—or somehow patch over the crevices that had gaped open in her well-loved landscape these past twenty-four hours. She was powerless to do so. There was no going back . . . only forward. She'd continue through the day, fulfill her obligations, and hope that somehow the cool routine of the passing hours would put things back into perspective.

She tucked her completed charts into the cubbyhole above her desk.

"Will," she called tentatively, her voice sounding thin and nervous in her own ears.

"Yes, Kate?" The old man put down his pen and charts and waited for her to continue.

"You know, today is the day I'm scheduled to speak to that 4-H group over at Hickory High. Mike Lessing, the new principal, called to confirm, and I—"

"I remember, gal. I may be old but I'm not senile!" His grin erased the gruffness from his voice, and the discomfort from the morning. "I think you'll do a mighty fine job with that. The last speaker they sent down just about put those kids to sleep. Caught myself yawning a bit! You go ahead. I'm only going up to McNaughtly's to do a round of inoculations. Silly sheep. I'd much rather be working with cows—those big honest eyes, the warm, clean smell of 'em . . ." He narrowed his eyes and peered at her across the room. Kate hung on his words, knowing that deep

100

intense look often signaled a thought or a comment that she particularly cherished. Now his rough voice recommenced. "You know, Kate, they somehow remind me of you. You're both indiscriminate eaters!"

Kate smoothed her skirt over her slim hips and glanced nervously into the lopsided mirror hanging behind the school stage. To the students milling around and moving noisily to their places, Dr. Harrington was beautiful. But at this moment, with the unseasonable heat permeating the wings of the old high school auditorium and the queasy flutterings of her stomach, Kate didn't realize that at all. "Good grief!" she muttered deprecatingly, resting her palm against her cheek. "I'm scared! How silly! I've lectured in college, taken oral exams before a roomful of learned doctors, spoken before a conference of veterinarians from all over the state and—standing here before a class of high school sophomores—I'm shaking in my boots!" She tossed her dark head and scolded the reflection before her. Shape up, Harrington! These kids are nice and eager to hear about your work. They *asked* you to come! And you have mutual interests: horses, cows, pigs—and *anyone* who likes pigs can't be all bad!

Like an exclamation mark at the end of that thought, a buzz accompanied by an ear-splitting screech shot across the stage as Mike Lessing, the youthful principal, tested the microphone. Then Kate heard his amicable voice introducing the guest

101

speaker and honorary 4-H adviser, Dr. Katherine Harrington.

Kate stood straight and tall, shot one determined smile back into the mirror, and headed out onto the wide wooden stage. A sea of smiling faces greeted her, and Kate returned their welcome grins readily. Ignoring the scattered catcalls and whistles, she began to speak.

"President Truman once said that nobody should be president unless he has been around pigs . . . and a manure pile! Well, students, I don't know if I'll get any of you to run for president, but I sure am going to give you a chance to get knee-deep in the job requirements."

Appreciative laughter swept the room and then settled to a hush as she continued her lecture.

A wonderful sense of pleasure and pride bubbled within Kate. It *had* been a good idea all along. Look at those faces! And that boy over there nodding at her words. And the blond taking notes. She felt the students responding positively, enjoying her as she was enjoying them. She delighted in their interest, sparking her talk with anecdotes and jokes, and as she neared the end of her prepared lecture she decided to tell them the story of Molly the pig, its surgery, its struggle to survive, and how it had responded to the care of its owner.

"I know most of you have animals of some sort in your care," she concluded, "and will be raising others for the upcoming fair. Let me encourage you to—"

Her words were interrupted by a spattering of titters from the students near the side of the auditorium, and a sharp, mechanical clicking noise. Kate paused and looked about, wide-eyed, confused as the chuckles spread, then exploded into laughter. At that moment a movement near the lip of the stage caught her eye.

Trotting toward her from under the drawn curtain, she saw a mechanical pink pig, encumbered in its journey by a bit of white gauze wrapped around its middle. It rattled directly toward her, pink legs churning like pistons, head bobbing dumbly, its baby blue eyes rolling at the stage lights.

Too surprised to move, Kate stood stock-still while the toy pig circled her once, then came to a stop beside her. Even Kate could not help but laugh. It was ridiculous! Struggling to regain her composure and calm the audience before her, Kate bent over and gathered the pig in her arms. She clutched its thrashing legs with her free hand, grinned out at her audience, and said, "This is just one of the many facets of being a veterinarian—one is always on call!"

Amid the chortling laughter, she pulled free a slip of white paper stuck beneath the gauze and scanned its message:

Help! I think I'm in
love with you!

A blast of heat seared her face, and she could feel the blood rising above the soft neckline of her sweater, coloring her neck and cheeks. She turned

103

and peered off into the shadows of the wings. And then she saw him. Standing, watching her from the stage doorway, his lean, muscular frame filling the narrow space. Gray slacks, a pale blue shirt open at the collar, revealing a *V* of tan flesh shadowed by a mat of curling hair. The strong column of his neck, that square jaw, the wide smile, and those laughing blue eyes. Electric blue eyes. Those damn eyes!

As her heart pounded and her knees grew weak, she thought, It's not fair! Oh, body, behave!

Then her irascible nature took over. One dark brow lifted, she tilted her head and winked conspiratorially at her audience. "Looks like I've got *two* patients waiting—a pig . . . and a donkey! So if you'll excuse me, I'll see you all again next week." She added over the fond laughter and chatter, "Don't forget, I want to see completed charts on your daily care and feeding schedules! Dismissed."

Eyes narrowed, chin tilted at a threatening angle, she charged toward the waiting, watching figure. "Craig Turner! You . . . you . . ."

Laughing, Craig raised his open hands in a gesture of mock supplication. His rich voice embraced her. "Don't be mad, my beautiful Kate. It was an emergency. Damn pig is lovesick."

Kate stopped short right in front of him, facing him toe-to-toe, hands on hips, her storming eyes flashing danger into his cool blue ones. "Craig Turner! Take this thing!" She shoved the slippery pink pig against his broad chest. Loosened from her karate grip, it gave one rebellious mechanical wiggle, clicked, and fell silent.

With feigned sorrow, Craig placed it in a wooden crate on the floor and intoned woefully, "Poor pig. I think you've broken its heart."

"And that's not all I'd like to break!" Kate replied, repressing the grin that tugged at her rose-petal lips. Her eyes danced with an amusement she tried to hide.

But Craig, looking at her with blatant desire, read her clearly. "Ah, my beautiful Kate, you weren't supposed to meet my messenger of love until tonight . . . until there was wine and candlelight and I could explain properly. But . . . but I couldn't wait." He moved closer, slid his arms around her, and pressed his hands against the narrow curve of her back, pulling her close to him, his heat melting her through the frail barriers of their clothing. "I've got to leave—"

She felt what little strength she had left drain from her through her toes. "No . . . when?"

"Now. I have to. There are some things I've got to take care of, some plans I've got to get rolling for Jeremy."

"What kind of plans is Jeremy making?"

"Well"—he hesitated—"actually *I'm* making the plans." He saw the frown that immediately creased her brow, and laid a quick finger on her lips. "Now listen, I haven't got time to defend myself. This is *not* just another example of my incurably bossy nature. Please. Just trust me." His hands tightened on her back.

Kate leaned into him, her face tilted up, her dark eyes locked to his sky-blue ones. It felt delicious to lean just so, to let herself absorb his warmth. "All right. I'll trust you—for now."

"Kate, I'll—"

"Ahem!" An awkward cough and a burst of laughter shattered the moment. "No seducing on the school stage, if you please!"

Mike Lessing stood three feet away, arms akimbo, feet planted wide. "Will you look at this! Am I wrong, Turner? Or was it just about fifteen years ago that old man Hardridge, my beloved predecessor, found you in a scene somewhat reminiscent of this. With the A-squad varsity cheerleaders—all seven of them!"

"Lessing, you rat!" Craig's warm laughter bounced and ricocheted about the now-empty auditorium.

Mike winked at a now composed Kate, who stood between the two. "At least your taste has improved, Turner."

"But not your timing, Lessing! Always getting a foul just when I'm about to score—"

"And Jeremy clearing the way for you . . . blocking anything in sight!"

The two men grinned at the memories and the moment. Then Craig slipped an arm back around Kate's waist. She grinned teasingly up into his handsome face, pried his hand from her side, and dropped it.

"I think I'd better let Mike fill me in on the other assorted details of your past." She pivoted toward the shorter man, tossed her hair back from her face, and quipped, "Was it really the entire cheerleading squad, Mr. Principal?"

Before Mike could answer, Craig caught her from behind, wrapping his arms around her shoulders, bending his knees until his body molded to hers. He rested his chin on the sensitive hollow between her collarbone and throat. "Kate . . . Craig Turner has no past! He was never alive until last night. Never lived, never breathed, never felt anything before." He paused for a second, his breath a warm, thrilling whisper against her ear. Then his hands dropped from her flesh and he stepped away. "I've got to go." He shook his head, frowning, fighting to find the right words, any words to say here and now, with others around. His eyes clouded, darkened. "I'm running late now. I've got to go, Kate. But I'll be back. 'Bye, Kate. 'Bye, Mike."

She watched the lean figure lope to the door.

Again, over his shoulder, " 'Bye, Kate."

And to the empty doorway, a whispered "Goodbye Craig."

CHAPTER FIVE

Priscilla raced across the slick, metallic surface of the operating table, took a flying leap, and landed with all twenty needle-sharp claws extended on Kate's shoulder. The earsplitting yowl of a frantic Siamese filled the small office.

"Oh, my lovely Puss, my poor, lovely Puss. Is that nasty doctor hurting my baby?" Mrs. Garvey, a matronly woman with blue hair, rushed to Kate's side and attempted to pluck the terrified cat from its precarious perch.

"It's all right, Mrs. Garvey. Perhaps if you'd wait in the other room, Puss would be less distracted!" Kate reached up, and with sure, calm movements, removed the clawing cat and held it firmly on the table. There had been a slight edge to her voice, and the older woman, surprised, edged meekly from the room.

Kate shook her head as the door closed. "Don't know what's gotten into me, Puss." She eyed the now docile cat with a thoughtful expression. "I'm really not mad, you know. I'm not the type. Especially with sweet beasts like you."

"Oh, Priscilla"—she stroked the now purring Siamese—"how much simpler to be a cat. Purr when I'm happy, spit and hiss when I'm not . . . And *that's* just what I'd like to do now!" She slapped her hand sharply on the metal table, causing every single hair on the cat's back to leap to attention.

With a self-mocking grin, she smoothed the startled cat, and let her thoughts race. Why, Kate Harrington, that's just how you're acting—like a cat in heat! Pacing about, a bundle of nerves, just trembling with desire. Your fur all on edge, your skin all ablaze with the thought of his touch stroking you. Oh, shame on you, girl! Do you think that man is lying sleepless at night? Turning himself inside out all day long over you? Bet your boots he's not!

She laughed deep in her throat, a mixture of frustration, exasperation, and humor. Again Priscilla did a panicked, backward dance toward the edge of the table. "Come on, Puss, at least we can fix what ails you. Now, if only my problems were that easy to solve."

But they weren't. She heard his laugh on the breeze, smelled his scent in the pines, and felt his presence in the warm cabin whenever she snuggled down beneath the heavy quilts in the wide, empty wooden bed.

Will never mentioned Craig. It was as if he had never come back, except that Kate could see the effects of his visit etched in the deep lines of the old man's face. Arie kept her own hopes private and carefully steered Kate away from the subject. As for Kate, she was *glad* he hadn't been around the last couple of days. She needed this time to iron out the wrinkles he had caused, to pull her life back onto its peaceful, uncomplicated course. But try as she might, that tranquillity was artfully avoiding her grasp.

There was no denying her attraction to Craig, to that one man who had set her atremble, ignited the fires so long banked and tamed. Craig Turner. The laughing look of his eyes, the way his thighs moved in his jeans, the curves and planes of his body, seen, touched, just that once yet etched permanently on her mind and fingertips.

She worked at fever pitch all day, plunging herself into her work—taking the earliest calls, the late emergencies—anything to wear herself out. Last evening she'd stayed for supper at the house in town, lingering over chitchat with Will and Arie. Later, back at the cabin, she'd paced and turned, crossing and recrossing the floor, and finally she'd called Ginger and followed the plume of her tail through the underbrush and up the mountain paths, seeking and absorbing the mountain's quiet . . . the peace, the tranquillity. They ended up at Jeremy's clearing, where they sat in the long shadows of the pines and basked in the lovely, sensuous strains of dulcimer music.

Kate felt at ease in Jeremy's casual company, and besides . . . he was lonely, too.

Jeremy told her stories, stories about himself and Craig in another time: bareback races across the plowed fields, days spent playing hooky from school to catch frogs and tree peepers that made their inevitable way to the teacher's desk, and how the three freshmen, Mike Lessing included, had crashed the senior prom dressed up like girls, replete with wigs and padded bras—and Jeremy had been wooed by the captain of the football team.

Kate laughed till her sides hurt. Jeremy fed sweetly aromatic branches of laurel to the fire, and Ginger growled at the crackle and pop of the heated sap. Sips of sour mash. The heady fragrance of the fire. Jeremy's tongue spinning stories from the past.

"That kid was fascinated by everything—people, politics, horses, and babies. Not to mention sawmills, ukuleles, computers, and the control panel of anything that moved. And he was always a rebel. That was the problem. He had an opinion on everything, would try anything. And if he was wrong, if it didn't work—well, he was the first to admit it. But folks don't take to that around here. Folks in Hickory Ridge don't go much for that sort of thing. Maybe if his dad had stood up for him, been on *his* side, but . . ." Jeremy shrugged and fell silent, poking at the flames with the charred stub of a stick.

"Why didn't he, Jeremy? I know Will. He's a good man."

"Sometimes it's easy to be good to everyone but your own." He looked up, his brows drawn in a dark line. "I'm not faultin' Will Turner. I just don't think he could ever quite figure Craig out—"

"Can you?"

"Maybe," he answered with a lopsided grin. "The stars tell me. You know those Aquarians . . . they're kind of like the ocean. Deep and tranquil beneath those layers and waves of rebellion and humor."

"What a lovely way to describe a person," Kate had answered.

"Oh, I'm just a poet at heart." He laughed shyly, then added, "And I'm especially fond of the ocean." Jeremy's voice dropped almost to a whisper. "I was headin' for the ocean when I lost my leg. Right there on the beach. Heard the grenade go off but didn't feel a thing. I was so close to goin' home."

"Oh, Jeremy," she breathed, chills lifting the hairs on her arms and neck. "Oh, Jeremy . . ."

"Hey, it's okay—"

"Is it? Are you all right here? Will you be able to manage for the winter?"

"Probably not. But Craig's taking care of that now. He's off making some arrangements, a grand design for my future!"

"Oh, Jeremy," she protested, locking her arms tightly around her knees. "I'd just hate to have someone manage *my* life."

"I hate it also, Kate."

112

She spun toward him, her eyes wide with remorse. "I know you do. I'm sorry, Jeremy. I wasn't thinking."

"Yes, you were, Kate. But you were thinking about you. And we're in two different situations. Believe me, it took awhile to get used to. It's harder than doing it yourself—that dependence. And"—Jeremy flashed a crooked grin—"sometimes the guy can be a bit overbearing. But Kate, Craig's always there when I need him. Kind of like the Lone Ranger."

Kate had smiled and nodded and lowered her eyes. If Jeremy could see that clearly into Craig's soul, could he read her secrets as well? Was the molten core of her desire obvious to those gentle eyes? To *everyone's* eyes? To Will? And Arie? And . . . ? The thought caused her hands to shake.

Kate thought of Jeremy's words as she dropped on to a brightly cushioned chair and looked around the now empty reception area. "Well, Arie, what's next? Don't tell me I might have some breathing space?"

"Wish that were what it meant, Kate. I know you need some rest." Arie's eyes were soft and affectionate. She could see from the faraway look in the young woman's eyes that Kate had become inextricably enmeshed in the Turner family's tensions. She had watched Kate closely since Craig's arrival and recognized the telltale signs of strain and yearning. And what was worst of all, Arie knew there wasn't a thing she could do about it.

Instead she resumed in her most businesslike

113

voice, "No, Kate, no rest for a while. Will phoned in while you were with the Garveys' cat and asked me to cancel all the afternoon appointments. He sounded worried, Kate. Said he'd seen two more cases of sick horses today—"

Kate shuddered. That made three days in a row Will had been called out to check on horses in the surrounding counties. All the symptoms were ominously similar. And now it had them both very concerned. "That's bad news, Arie—"

"I know, dear. Let's pray to the good Lord that it's not EIA. Will doesn't need an epidemic on his hands right now, on top of everything else." Her disconsolate voice trailed off, then resumed with renewed vigor. "Probably t'isn't anything at all. But Will did want you to make rounds with him this afternoon. He had two more calls to make out at horse ranches. Said he thought it was time you participated."

Before Kate had a chance to reply, their conversation was cut short by the sound of Will's truck, lurching to a noisy stop in front of the clinic. He came in just long enough to collect some fresh medical supplies—and Kate—and then both headed back to the hills. They rode in companionable silence, both absorbing strength from the passing landscape, a soothing balm for the soul. The multicolored blend of grassy pasture land, backswept into majestic stands of pines, fields, and hills that rolled and curved around barns and sheds were all showered in high fall sunshine. Kate glanced over at Will and smiled at the familiar sparkle that lit his eyes as he moved ahead to

114

the work he loved. The work they both loved. During their many calls there was little time to ponder her problems, and Kate was relieved to have her mind so thoroughly occupied by problems totally unrelated to Craig Turner.

It was early evening when Will and Kate threw their bags in the back of the truck. They had just completed calls at two ranches at the edge of the county. The horses—one on one ranch, three on the second—all appeared fevered and restless, short of breath . . . just downright sick. Will and Kate took blood samples from all four, packaged them carefully, and warned both farmers to keep the horses isolated from the rest of their animals until they got the test results. Caution was eating away at his fading optimism.

"Ah." Will's voice was thick with weariness. "Day is done . . . at last."

"Let me drive, Will. You haven't had a chance to relax since dawn." Kate walked over to the driver's side of the cab, and Will shifted obediently to the passenger seat. His eyes were half-closed, and in the fading light of the sun, his set face, the sharp strong profile, the web of wrinkles patterning his skin all seemed quite dear to her. Again she realized how much this caring, stubborn old man had come to mean in her life.

The truck jolted to a halt in front of the clinic. "Stay for dinner, Kate?" Will asked. "Knowing that appetite of yours, you must be darn near starvation."

Kate chuckled. "That, dear Will, I am. But I can't forget dinner for poor Ginger—and I could use a long soak in a hot tub. Think I'll pass tonight. But thanks, Doc." Suddenly she leaned over and planted a kiss on his roughened skin. "Get some sleep, Will, I have a feeling tomorrow is going to be another long day."

"Hah! Look who's giving the orders now." He snapped in an effort to distract Kate's attention from the blush that had spread across his face. "Give a woman an inch, and she'll take over your life!"

With a wave he disappeared inside the clinic doors, and Kate headed for the center of town, her mind concentrating on dog food, mushroom omelettes, and a cool glass of chablis. As quickly as her weary limbs could propel her, she gathered together two sacks of groceries, made the obligatory small talk with Tom, the supermarket checker, and headed across the street to her jeep.

As she stepped down from the curb her eye was caught by a cloud of dust rising from around the curve in the road. The haze from the spiraling fog whirled closer, obscured her vision for a moment, and in seconds she was forced back onto the sidewalk by the screech of wheels and the speed of a passing vehicle. Peering from behind the barrier of her bundles, Kate saw a gleaming, spanking-new pickup fly by, pulling an equally gleaming, metallic Air Stream trailer. It whizzed past her like a silver bullet and on up the curve of the street, climbing toward the mountains.

Kate coughed as the dust settled on her lips and

clogged her lungs. "Crazy driver! Tourist! Go back to Disneyland!"

Wearily, Kate deposited her parcels in the back of the jeep and began the trek up the mountain. She spent the first few miles muttering to herself about wild drivers, backache, piglets, and other problems. But as her mind cleared, her senses became more and more alert and attuned to the beauty around her. The stillness. The sharp tang of approaching winter carried on the evening breeze. The murmuring of the wind in the branches along the road. The flash and flicker of color—bird, mouse, chipmunk, deer—glimpsed along the fringes of the woods. She drew in a huge breath, held it locked tight within her lungs, her shoulders raised and tense, then blew it out in a long, cleansing breath. "Ah! This is why I am here," she whispered to no one at all. "Ah, yes . . . now I remember!"

The sun had slipped serenely behind the slopes, painting the forests in a palette of emerald and azure, sapphire and ebony. Rich colors, deep and silent, soothing. The forest floor dimly glimpsed, a carpet of drying grass and fallen leaves, bare saplings. The constant solid thrust of the trunks, rough textured or smooth, bent or lodge-pole straight. The canopy of branches woven, interlocked, a filigree laced against a darkening sky.

Kate breathed lightly now, her hands loose on the wheel, the jeep finding its own way home in the twilight.

Turning into her drive, Kate found more than she

had expected. The trailer was parked there, its cold, metallic bulk blocking one side, with just enough space left over for her to maneuver the jeep to a halt.

Leaping from behind the wheel, Kate raced to her door. It was still locked, and behind it she heard Ginger's frantic barking; was just reaching into her pocket for her key when two iron-strong arms grabbed her from behind. In the same moment, her mind registered the power of the man behind her, the familiar muskiness of his scent, the harsh, identifying purr of his voice.

"Oh, God, woman, how I've missed you!"

It was Craig.

She turned within the circle of his arms, leaning her weight back against his hold. His hands pressed tight against the small of her back, pressing her to him, then moved down over the curve of her buttocks, lifting her to him, hungrily. Kate began to protest, but his mouth was moving over hers, his lips warm and urgent, parted with the pressure of his kiss. Their teeth bumped together, and she laughed against his mouth in joy and desire. And his tongue began to search the silken lining of her mouth, probing, tasting, circling her tongue and leading it back into his mouth. His hungry mouth nibbled at the outline of her lips and across her cheek, nuzzling into the spill of dark hair over her ear. With her rising laughter she felt the hard force of him rising against her and felt her own throbbing passion. Somewhere in the foggy distance she heard Ginger barking frantically, and Kate finally opened her eyes and dared to speak. "Craig—"

"In the flesh, woman. Very much in the flesh." He rubbed his rough cheek against her smooth one, sending sparks flying through her body.

Kate unclasped her hands from around his neck and slowly drew her palms, one on either side of his head, slowly across the thick tangle of his hair. Ruffling it, feeling the smooth, curved bone of his skull, her fingertips traced the fine shape of his head. Her hands were tight and trembling, drawn so slowly down to his jaws, until she held his face in her hands with the rough shadow of his afternoon growth prickling against her palm. His cheeks were cool but his eyes ablaze. His lips were still parted and his breathing shallow and ragged.

"Craig?" Her voice coated his name with honey, but her eyes were flashing with mischief. "Craig, what is that damn thing doing parked in my driveway?"

"*My* driveway."

"*Our* driveway? Why is it here?"

"Well, you said I needed to slow down, to wait. And a man might as well wait in style."

"But where did it come from?"

"Bought it in Roanoke. Got a great deal, complete with dishes, towels, and a shower curtain."

"But what are you going to *do* with it?"

"Sleep in it. Unless you have, ah . . . better ideas? Miss me that much?"

"Not *that* much."

119

His lips curved in a fierce smile. "Well, tell me you're glad to see me."

Kate laughed. "I thought that was fairly obvious!"

"Tell me anyway."

"Why?" she teased, lifting onto tiptoe as if to better look into his sea-blue eyes and managing at the same time to slide her slim hips up across the drawn bow of his body.

Craig groaned and buried his face in her neck. "Oh, Kate, you feel so good. I've missed you."

"Well, I haven't had to roll anyone down the mountainside in the last three days. I guess I've missed you, too."

A low, exultant laugh rumbled in his throat. "Knew it, Kate! You had to; damn, you just had to! And now, woman, let's let that poor doggie out before she tears down the door. Come on!" And with a wide grin he let her slip from his arms.

Ginger spilled through the doorway like a puddle of honey, landing at Kate's feet and thrashing about in wild, protective wiggles. She gave Craig a quick once-over, found him to be perfectly satisfactory, then ran barking to the bundles left forgotten in the back of the jeep.

Craig carried them in, balancing them, along with Kate's heavy black veterinary bag in his strong arms. He had seen how tired she was. Now, after the first moments of their greeting, he had let his eyes linger on her, trying to slake the yearning that had consumed him these past days, and he had seen her weariness. Seen that her dark eyes glowed even darker, shadowed by fatigue, that she had grown a bit thinner, the lovely bones of her face more finely sculpted beneath her translucent skin. It tore him apart.

"Sit down, Kate," he ordered, his gruffness surprising them both. "Sit down. There, by the hearth. I'll have a fire going for you in a second."

"Let me just start some supper," she offered, turning toward the kitchen.

"No you don't!" He caught her in his arms and led her to the overstuffed armchair with its worn ottoman. "Put your feet up. Just rest. Here"—he grabbed a copy of Thoreau off the bookshelf and tossed it on her lap—"read!"

Kate nodded and opened the book in her lap. But her disobedient eyes drifted from the pages and she watched his muscles roll and flex beneath his flannel shirt when he pulled off his sheepskin jacket and tossed it on the couch. Watched his hard, lean body move within his clothes as he strode to the kitchen and disappeared. Kate could hear the clatter of Craig and Ginger in the kitchen, his low, rumbling voice, the dog's answering bark . . . the soft, sibilant whisper of the wind outside her windows . . . Her eyelids drooped, closed, her head sank back against the warm, curved back of the chair.

"Ready to come back to me, darlin'?" His rugged face broke into a smile as she opened her eyes.

"M-m-m-m, what do I smell?"

"Omelettes. Cheese and tomato and ham—and

some muffins I found in your freezer. And a glass of Craig Turner's world-famous mulled wine."

"Craig, you are an angel!"

"Wait, woman. Later I'll show you my other side."

Later, he did. But first they had eaten and watched the fire and talked.

"Where have you been, Craig? Where do you go when you're not here?"

"Home." He laughed. "I've got a place north of here. Up at the very top of the state. A pretty place. You'd like it."

"A farm?" she prompted, wanting to know more.

"Sort of." He slid his eyes away to the fire and concentrated on the popping of the sparks, then acquiesced and added, "I have horses."

"Horses? We happen to be in the midst of a horse problem right now. I only hope it doesn't get serious."

"My guess is that *you* take everything about your work seriously."

"Yes, I do, Craig. Don't you?"

He paused. "No, not everything, Kate. There are parts of my business I don't give very much of myself to. They're there . . . and they do well for me"—he laughed harshly—"but I don't like them a whole lot."

"The horses?" Kate ventured hesitantly, detecting an ominous tone in his voice.

"No, Kate, not the horses. The land I told you about."

"You mean the land you sold?"

"Yes. Sold it and took the cash to buy my own place, and my horses." His eyes left her face and traveled over the still room. "Or at least I thought I had. Damndest thing. My lawyer retained the mineral rights for me—standard operating procedure, he explained later. And they found oil. You can guess the rest."

The regret in his tone touched her, and she sought to recapture his glance. "I'd rather not guess, Craig. Please tell me what happened then."

"Then I was suddenly a very rich man. Disowned. But rich."

How well she could understand what a two-edged sword that money must have been.

She let her cheek fall onto the back of one hand, and held his eyes. "So you're here to try and make peace now? Good! I knew I felt a heart beating beneath that hot exterior!"

"Glad you felt it! Because the second reason I came back was that I find it damn near impossible to stay away from *you!*"

He slid from his seat and knelt at the foot of her chair, his arms resting across her thighs, his flat, hard stomach against her knees, his eyes blazing into hers. "I couldn't stay away. Tried and couldn't. Knew I should but couldn't." She could feel the heat of his body entering her legs, rising to the top of her thighs, to her womb, centering there in the secret hollow at the center of her being. And she felt herself melt and grow weak.

"Craig, I—"

His kiss stifled her words, stoppered her breath, and tore the air from her lungs when he pulled his mouth away. "Come here, darlin'. There's a place I want to take you. Come with me."

Reaching for her hand, he stood and drew her up beside him; refusing to explain, he pulled on his jacket, helped her bundle into hers, tossed her mittens, a hat, a scarf from the closet, and led her out into the clear, sparkling night.

He did a quick dash into the interior of the trailer, and came back laden with a rolled sleeping bag and a shiny red sphere strapped across his back.

"What in the world is that?" Kate asked.

"Sleeping bag."

"No, you turkey," she chortled, banging her head playfully into his side. "Your red ball there—"

"Telescope, woman. Don't leave home without one." He shifted his grip, flicked on the beam of a small flashlight, and wrapped his free arm around her waist. "Come on, we're going up!"

When they came to the end of the trail Craig had chosen, Kate caught her breath in delight. An enormous boulder, catapulted from the summit during some long-ago cataclysm, lay just a few feet from the face of the mountain. Before it was a clearing, a hollow scooped out of the mountainside and covered with a soft blanket of pine needles and leaves. Beyond it was the sky. Star-spangled, an endless sweep of blue velvet splashed with diamond dust.

"See there? There are the Seven Sisters. And over

there—the Pleiades. Do you see that star cluster there? Look . . . no wait, let me set this up . . . Now! Now look through here."

The stars sprang into scintillating luminescence across Kate's field of vision. " 'The white radiance of eternity' " she murmured, quoting a poem she had been assigned to memorize in high school. The line had never held any real meaning for her until now.

"That's nice," Craig murmured in her ear. "So you love the stars, too, oh, heavenly maiden?" His lips nibbled around to the hollow at the base of her throat.

"Stop, Craig. I'm trying to concentrate. I think I've found Orion."

Enjoying her intensity, Craig laughed softly to himself and sank down upon the down-filled sleeping bag. His eyes traveled hungrily over the shape of her, the colors and textures of her skin and hair and lips, lit now by the white wash of moonlight and star beams. He sat just so for a while, satisfied by her nearness and her beauty. Then he grew hungry for the sound of her voice. "Kate . . ."

She turned and looked down at him. "What?" Her dark brows furrowed above her luminous eyes. Her face was painted with an ethereal, lambent beauty.

"Talk to me—" He swallowed, his chest rising and falling heavily. "Tell me something."

His passion was contagious. It leapt from his body to hers, devouring her, consuming her. She answered with the same counterfeit calm. "You mean you want to have a conversation—*now?*"

Craig laughed. His arm caught her, pulling her down across his body, her weight settling lightly on his chest and hips, her hair falling like a curtain of smoke about his face. His kisses moved down the sweeping line of her forehead to the tip of her straight, fine nose, lingered playfully, then attacked her waiting, eager mouth. There the playfulness disappeared, vanquished by the intensity of their matched ardor. Their tongues were impassioned explorers, questing, hunting, probing, delving into the delicious recesses of each other's mouths, skimming the surfaces of sweet, moist lips, then plumbing the silken depths again.

His hands tangled in the spill of Kate's smoke-dark hair, and he tipped her head back, drawing his rasping tongue down in search of the flickering pulse in her throat. Found it and nuzzled there, his lips pressed to the beat of her blood.

Kate hung poised there, reed-slim body arched above him, feeling his mouth on her pulse, and aware of the long length of him pressed beneath her. Her body was weightless; her bones dissolved; only her flesh was alive, moist, heated, aware. Yes! They were two whole separate sentient beings enmeshed in the webbing of each other's nerve endings and sensations.

She felt fragile and rare, a dark orchid pressed to his breast. And his hands stroked her hair, her shoulders, her back, as if he, too, found her rare and precious. His hands memorized her shape, her form, the silken texture of her skin. His mouth trailed kisses

126

across her throat and, nuzzling beneath the neckline of her sweater, he sought the pendulant curve of her breast.

Kate's body trembled like a branch in the breeze, and a low moan escaped her lips.

That soft, purring sound excited Craig more than anything else could have. With erupting fervor, he heaved his torso off the yielding down, Kate still in his arms, pivoted on his hip and knee, and lay her quivering body beneath him. The flat, hard wall of his chest pressed against her pliant breasts. His mouth dusted her with a rain of kisses; sharp, nipping kisses that stung and excited.

For a split second Kate pushed him away and lay there, looking up at this lean, fierce man with his hair the color of autumn leaves and his wolf-blue eyes . . . for a moment she hesitated.

And Craig saw the reluctant desire smoldering in her eyes . . . and felt it, too. Knew he should stop. Knew he had never had so much at risk. But she was so lovely, so warm and tempting with those dark, serious eyes, all luminous and full of promise. "Oh, Kate . . . my beautiful Kate. I couldn't sleep at night thinking about you, couldn't get through the days—"

Her husky, delighted laughter startled him, but when she laced her slender arms and legs around his tensed frame, he forgot everything but the feel of her . . . and the moment.

His hands traced the outline of her body, slid beneath the hem of her sweater, his fingertips gliding up across the smooth skin of her stomach, across the fragile framework of her ribs. His eager fingers brushed the lower curve of her breasts, and his throat constricted in a rush of excitement.

Kate's own breath was trapped in her throat, and then, with another soft purr, she nudged her way to one side, arched her back, and slipped her sweater quickly over her head. The cold night air bit her on the shoulders, but Craig was already pulling the folds of the double-sized sleeping bag up over them.

He stopped long enough to shed his own shirt and pants, and paused, searching those glowing, moonlit eyes. Her lips edged into a smile. And he reached down and unfastened the waistband of her slacks, drew them down over the curve of her hips along with the unseen silk of her panties, and slid down along her body to edge off her boots—and left her lying, long and naked, in their warm, dark love cave.

Slowly, slowly he began to make his way back up her body. His fingertips and lips trailed along her insteps, circled her ankles and up her calves, and slid so lightly, but with maddening arousal, along the inside of her thighs . . . over the soft, delicately changing course to trace the fine arc of her hipbones, the sweet tuck of her waist. Resting his cheek on the soft curve of her belly, he lay still a moment, feeling her writhe and tremble beneath him. Her hands fluttered madly across his back, caressing, stroking, raking erratic patterns over the wide span of his back. He rubbed his cheek playfully against her belly and felt the muscles there just beneath the skin tighten

128

and ripple. Her fingers found his face, and he caught two fingertips between his teeth, trapped them with a gentle bite, and rasped the sensitized tips with his rough tongue. Kate arched against him, stirring and tossing in the confines of the sleeping bag. Their body warmth filled the interior as with touch and taste they stoked their own private furnace. . . .

Kate wanted him. She felt the growing heat of their snug cocoon rise along with the heat of her own blood. She loved the feel of him, the taste and scent of his heated body. The sure gentleness of his hands, the openness of his desire. She liked knowing he wanted her! Liked the little thrill of power it gave her. She moved against him, letting her hips circle in that old, sweet dance of desire. Felt him straining hard and hungry against her. And gathering his head in her hands, she urged him up, up to her breasts, and cried soft love words in her throat when he found her, when his mouth circled teasingly, tentatively, around the fullness of her breasts, his tongue painting narrower and narrower circles until at last it rasped across her taut and straining nipples. He took her heart-swelling nibs in his mouth and nibbled, sucked, and nipped until Kate knew she would explode . . . so steaming, seething, burning with excitement were her senses. Her hands stroked him, playing urgently across every part of him she could reach, inciting him and rousing him to madness, until his senses were whipped to a frenzy and he had to love her: "Got to love you, darlin'." The words were torn from his throat and he felt her welcome him, and they were one, together . . . united in ecstasy, his length filling her, carrying her up, up off this mountainside until she soared among the star-blazed heavens . . . and she carried him with her, soaring, exploding, bursting in a light to rival any star.

Their descent was slow, dreamy, and delicious, and they lay for a while in each other's arms, the folds of the sleeping bag wrapped around them from head to toe, basking in each other's warmth and scent and quiescent passion.

Kate woke slowly, roused by the brisk air ruffling her hair, the unfamiliar warmth of Craig's solid body folded along hers. She felt all soft and shimmering, with no awareness of time or place outside of now and here. It had been more lovely than anything she had imagined. Letting her eyes adjust a moment to the moon-hazed darkness, she turned softly to him.

And suddenly the tears sprang to her eyes, brimming, spilling silently out of the corners of her dark, luminous eyes and into her hair. Craig lay asleep with a complete unfathomable remoteness in his beauty that made her want to cry out—to catch him in her arms and to have him again—to force open his eyes and see herself reflected in their sky-blue depths, her image filling his eyes, his soul. But instead he lay there locked away from her, silent, still, closed to her. Kate felt as though something in the center of her body had been punctured, as if she had been punched in the stomach.

"Craig? Craig? What have you done to me? Who are you . . . who . . . ?"

Her anguished murmur woke him. Sleep drained from his eyes, leaving the irises dark and flat, thoughtful and watchful. He lifted one bare arm, covered with dark, soft hairs, and touched her wet cheek. Then his wide hand passed over the curve of her body, once, gently, without passion but with tenderness and a sort of regret.

"Are you sorry, Kate? Don't be sorry."

"No, Craig. I'm not. I . . . I just . . . Suddenly you seemed very much a stranger. There is so much about you I don't know, don't understand. How will all this end?"

Craig gazed at her with a strange, weary yearning, wanting her more than he had ever wanted anyone. Yet he was balanced precariously at the brink of a confrontation he dreaded. Having kept himself locked tight for so long, having held himself in check with a tight rein, he was afraid to be vulnerable. Afraid to let himself loose.

In one restless, tensed movement, he slid from the sleeping bag and stood naked and beautiful in the night. Kate watched him; saw him pull on his clothes, disappear into them. And calmly, quietly, she, too, dressed.

CHAPTER SIX

The following days and nights fused together in a blur. But permeating it all was that timeless night spent at Star Gazing Rock. Kate tucked the memory inside herself, cherished it as one did a prized possession, then tried desperately to focus on the reality of her days, rather than the fantasy of that night. She needed time to sort through the emotions that tumbled about her. But Craig Turner, homesteading outside her cabin door, was definitely *not* a fantasy—and he made the task a most formidable one.

His knock brought her to the door one chilly November evening.

"Hi there, sweet Kate." He was dressed in flannel shirt, jeans, and heavy boots, looking almost as good as he had undressed.

"Hi there, yourself."

"Listen, things are freezing on the mountain, and I've brought Jeremy down. Join us for dinner?"

"Love to. Can I bring anything?"

"Just your beautiful self." He grinned, sliding a hand around the shawl collar of her sweater. He bent and kissed her, then let his cheek rest a moment against her hair. "I've missed being with you, babe."

Without answering, Kate pressed her palm against his cheek. She shifted her weight away from the door frame and let her bones and flesh melt into his. She was tingling down to the very soles of her boot-clad feet.

"Ummm . . . you smell like the forests, Mr. Turner."

"And you smell like the wind that whispers through my branches, Dr. Harrington." He turned his whole face into the dark fall of her hair. "With a touch of woodsmoke."

"I was baking. An apple cream pie. Interested?"

"Not now, baby. Food's definitely not what's on my mind."

"I thought you said Jeremy was waiting . . . ?"

Craig drew back, eyed her hungrily, and grinned. "Sure 'nuf." He turned to go and stopped. "Hey, why don't you bring that pie with you!"

Dinner was fun for them all. They sat scrunched, knees pressed against knees, around Craig's small table. They laughed, polished off a six pack, and laughed some more. "The Three Musketeers," Jeremy dubbed them.

"Keeping each other company during the long,

133

cold winter," Kate teased, glad to focus on such innocent companionship, and wishing she could settle for
only that from Will Turner's renegade son.

The two men looked at each other across the tiny
tabletop.

"Sorry, Kate, but I won't be here. I'm headin'
north."

"What? But you didn't even tell me."

"Didn't know"—he laughed—"until Craig told
me!"

"Just like that?" Kate didn't even know why she
was angry. "I mean, that's crazy. One minute you're
here, among friends who love you, and the next
you're on your way to God knows where—or Craig
Turner knows where, as the case may be!"

"What are you so riled up about, Kate? Jeremy's
going to be just fine. He'll be doing something important—"

"Something *you* arranged—"

"Yes, I arranged it, but that doesn't mean anything's wrong with it. He's perfect for the job, and
the job is perfect for him!"

"*You* say so."

"You're damn right I do."

"Hey! Hold it, you two! I'm the guy leaving! Remember me? Well, I'm not fussin', so how about if we
have another beer, and you two can fight, or make
up, or fight *and* make up, whatever, after I'm gone!"

They didn't fight, and there was really nothing to
make up about. It hadn't really been Jeremy's leaving they were arguing about at all. And later, as Craig

134

walked her back across the drive to the cabin, their breath mingling and rising in gray plumes against the black night air, Kate had felt the heat of his body mix with that of her own passion, and she had fled quickly behind the dubious security of her cabin door.

And at the clinic the next day, Kate's worries took but another turn. It had been a week filled with long, tiring hours as unrest grew among the neighboring horse farms. Will tried to fight off the unsettling apprehension, but it was evident in his eyes and coated the long periods of silence he fell into as he worked feverishly in the clinic. Kate and Arie were apprehensive, too, and worried daily about the possibility of serious contagion among the county's horse population.

Today, Kate thought as she slipped down on a chair beside her kitchen table that Tuesday morning. Today we should get the Coggins test results. And hopefully be able to do more than take blood samples . . . and try to calm nervous farmers. She picked at her eggs and looked out at the gray morning light leaking through the branches. But do what? Although they purposely avoided speaking about it, they all knew if the Coggins test confirmed equine infectious anemia, or "swamp fever" as the farmers referred to it, the infected horses would have to be put down . . . would have to be killed. *Horses down.* The very words caused a dull ache in Kate's stomach, and she tried to dispel the depressing thoughts as she swallowed a long drink of hot coffee. Ginger nestled comfortably at her feet, and she absently patted her head, slipping a piece of bacon between her waiting jaws.

She felt the gust of cold air before hearing the footsteps, but in a moment Craig stood in the kitchen doorway, clad in his usual faded jeans and warm shirt, a jacket slung over one shoulder. Her heart pounded as his smile warmed the room and came to rest on her face.

"Hope I didn't scare you, Kate. I'm out of coffee and couldn't quite face the day without it. . . ."

Kate smiled. "I've plenty, Craig. Sit down." She moved quickly to the coffeepot and was back with a filled mug as Craig settled down across from her. With a playful glint in his eye he had helped himself to her heaping plate of eggs and was devouring the creamy morsels post-haste. Kate slapped his hand playfully, and filled another plate. Her eyes lingered on his strong, angular features and she found herself again missing the intimacy they had shared, missing the touch of his body against her own. Missing the warmth of his embrace and the taste of his lips and the incredibly wondrous feeling he had freed within her.

"Nice . . ." Craig murmured.

Kate felt the burn in her cheeks immediately. "Wh . . . what?"

"Nice. The eggs." His eyes laughed, and she was convinced of her transparency in the presence of this bewitching man. "Craig, what gets you up so early today? These are vet's hours, you know." There. A

136

neutral subject. A chance to get back on a safe plane once again. But a shadow passed over Craig's face, and Kate was unexplainably sorry she had asked.

"Oh, I have some business to take care of before I return to my place."

"Will?" Kate's voice was hopeful. As far as she could tell, father and son had not yet spent any time together. "Can I be of any help?"

"No, not today. But soon. Today is something else. That oil business I told you about needs some attention."

Kate nodded. Desperately she wanted to turn the conversation back to Will, but she knew she couldn't. "Well, more coffee then? *That* I do well—"

"That and a hell of a lot more!" Craig's words were spontaneous, and Kate flushed at the outburst of emotion.

They both laughed, and Kate headed quickly toward the coffeepot. She was stopped midstep by the shrill ring of the telephone.

Kate stared at the phone. "Awfully early for phone calls." Finally she reached out and lifted the receiver. "Hello . . . Oh, no!" There was a pause while she listened intently. "Yes, of course, Arie. . . . No, I was about to leave, anyway. I'll go directly to the farm. And Arie—I'll take care of him, dear. Don't you worry."

The phone clicked dead, and Kate held it in her hand without moving, a dark shadow covering her face.

"My dad?" Craig's voice was low. "Is . . . is he all right?"

Kate had forgotten Craig was there, and his voice jerked her back to the present. "Oh, I'm sorry, Craig. Yes, Will is all right. As well as can be under the circumstances, I guess . . ." Her voice trailed off, and she began collecting warm boots and a jacket.

"Kate." Craig's voice was demanding now. "Where are you going?"

"To one of the horse farms. Will got the test results last night that we'd been waiting for. It *is* EIA. There're several horses on two farms that are infected." Her words slowed and stuck in her throat, but she forced them out. "They're going to have to be put down. Will is already on his way out . . . to get ready—"

"Oh, my God, that's a tough one." Craig rose and stuck his arms quickly through the sleeves of his thick jacket. "He can't do that alone. Come on, Kate—"

"Where are you going?"

"With you."

"But . . . but your business meeting . . ."

"It'll wait."

The two rode in silence, Kate maneuvering the heavy Land Rover along the narrow roads. Each was caught up in a pensive solitude but never unaware of the other's presence. Craig reached over and placed a reassuring hand on Kate's knee. "It's tough, but it'll be okay, Kate."

"You sound like you've been through this before."

138

Kate's voice was small and unsure . . . and filled with gratitude that Craig was there beside her.

"Yep. More than once. And every time I pray it'll be the last, even when I know, when I'm positive it's the only way . . . and the best thing for the horses. It's one of those potholes in life, Kate, that you can't walk around. Not in your business, not in mine. But at least maybe I can help carry you through it—"

Kate heard the gentleness in his voice. "And Will . . . ?"

"Yes. Maybe it is time."

They pulled into the farm gate just as full daylight reached the mountain peaks. The light was gray today, a dull, murky hue that hung above them and perfectly matched the spirits of the players in the dreaded drama. Silence lay over the field, broken only by the occasional nicker of a horse. Horses and owners had gathered at the far edge of the field, just past the thin, stark line of the fence. Five horses, the two farmers, and two young girls in jeans and sweaters. Silent. Waiting. And to one side a deep hole had been prepared in the field by a bulldozer. It kept filling up with mud and water, trying to level itself . . . almost as if in protest to what was about to happen.

Will was sitting in the clinic truck, waiting. He got out as they drove up.

For Kate, the next moments were filled with almost unbearable anguish. She saw Will's shoulders stoop and his steps slow under the weight of his pain.

139

Craig silently reached over and took the heavy veterinary bag from his father's hands.

Will showed neither surprise, nor anger, nor gratitude. The necessity—the rightness, the humaneness—of what had to be done here on the field overshadowed all personal emotions for the old vet.

"Mornin', Frank, Lou, Abigail, Marianne," Will greeted each of the people by name. His voice was hushed and solemn. The others only nodded. Kate crouched, opened the bag, and began to prepare the syringes. Thirty ccs of euthanasia solution in each. Five syringes, one for each horse. The thought made Kate's hands shake. Then all was ready.

And each horse, each beautiful, spirited horse, was led to the edge of the ditch. Will stood on one side of its head, its owner on the other, talking softly, soothing the dear animal, while Kate quickly injected the solution into its neck. Within seconds, each staggered and collapsed dead, shoved into the ditch as it fell.

The last horse was the hardest, led to the edge by the two girls. Their faces were twisted in agony, wet with tears, and Kate felt her own throat constrict, her eyes fill. When Will took hold of the rein, both girls began to wail aloud. The two farmers caught hold of the girls, pressing swollen faces to their rough jackets. Kate looked once in the mare's large brown eyes . . . and unbidden but unstoppable, the tears streamed down her face, and her body shook. Will reached out to her. But Craig was there. Placing his body like a shield between her and the horse, he pried the syringe from her fingers and plunged it home. The horse fell.

It was over. Five horses down.

The engine of the bulldozer coughed and sputtered, then the flat blade began to push the rich, dark earth over the grave. Will stood staring into the hole. Kate spoke softly to each of the farmers, watched the two girls, sobbing on each other's shoulders, weave their sad way toward the farmhouse, and turned back to her partner. But her eyes first found Craig. He was standing next to his father, watching her from over the older man's bowed head. Kate's lips quivered, and she smiled a weak smile, wanting nothing more than to run and hide in Craig's protective arms, lose herself there, shielded from the pain and sorrow of the world. And she could sense him wanting to do that for her. But her reason, her training held strong. Walking over steadfastly, she slipped an arm around Will's shoulder. "We'd best go back to the clinic, Will."

His worn, creased face turned to her. "That never gets any easier, Kate. Has to be done . . . and I try to think about all the healthy animals we're saving, but it doesn't make *this* any easier."

"Knowing you, Dr. Turner, it could never get easy. That's what I love about you."

Will looked away, brushed his hands against his work pants, and wiped a sleeve across his brow. "Are you okay, Katherine?"

"Sad . . . but okay, yes. I just hope those two girls will be all right."

"They will," the old vet said, squaring his shoulders. "That's the badge of the young. They can forget." And for the first time his eyes registered Craig's presence. With a mixture of regret, despair, and anger, his gaze traveled over his son's solemn, tight face. They stood locked in each other's stare, two sharpened edges of a blade, its point aimed straight at Kate's heart.

She stepped between the two men. "Come home, Will. It has been a long morning. I'll drive you back. Craig . . . Craig, will you—?"

"I'll bring the Rover. Go on."

Arie was waiting out in front of the clinic, her hands hidden in her pockets, a heavy, worn sweater thrown about her shoulders. "Come inside." She beckoned them toward the house. "I've got a pot of chowder and lots of hot coffee ready for you. I knew you'd need it."

Kate and Will dropped into chairs in the cozy living room where Arie had already prepared a fire. They sat silently, letting the heat seep into their chilled and tired bodies.

Kate heard the front door click open and shut, and looked up to see Craig standing there just inside the doorway. He bent and set the veterinary bag on the patterned rug, then straightened, the pull of his shoulders stretching open the collar of his jacket. For no reason Kate was immediately and totally aware of the strain of the heavy material across his chest . . . the way the jacket tapered to his narrow waist and rested there, emphasizing the jaunty aggressive angle of his hips. His hands were thrust deep in his pockets, one shoulder propped against the door frame. His face was an impassive mask: defiant, resolute. He had no smile for Kate, but his eyes lingered on her face and softened for a moment, dwelt softly on Arie, then traveled slowly over the familiar room, long unseen. Then his gaze hardened and returned to his father.

Will Turner spoke not a word. Glared across the room. Silent. Daring the younger man to speak first.

"Dad, I want to talk to you—"

"I've nothing to say to you. Why don't you go back to where you belong."

"I want to belong here, too. This is my home—"

"Was!"

"*Is.* There are things here I refuse to give up."

Will's eyes darted accusingly to Kate, and she felt the heat flood her cheeks.

"Don't look at Kate that way, Pop. She worries about you, cares about you. I've never met anyone so loyal."

"Certainly more loyal than my own son ever was."

"You asked too much, Pop."

"Too much? Is love too much? Respect? Honor? Is it too much to ask a son to share his father's hopes and dreams?"

"No. Not too much to *ask*. But you demanded it . . . demanded it all!"

"And got nothing!"

"Because there was never any in-between with

143

you. Never a compromise. I tried to talk to you, but you wouldn't listen. I wrote, but the letters came back unopened. I wanted to meet you halfway—"

"Only *after* you sold the land!"

"Yes. And I'm sorry. I'd undo that if I could. I'd give up my place, my horses, everything, to undo that now. But I can't. Besides, would it make any difference now?"

"None. You're nothing but a Judas Iscariot!"

"And your problem, Pop, is that you've always thought you were God!"

Kate's hand flew to her mouth.

"Enough!" Arie smacked the coffeepot back onto the table so hard the cups danced. "That is just enough. Craig Turner, you keep a rein on that temper of yours. And Will Turner, you old goat, listen to that boy and listen good. He's trying to speak from the heart."

Will harrumphed and dug his wiry old frame further into the old armchair.

"Now go on, Craig. You've got your father's undivided attention." Arie smiled angelically at both men.

"Pop. I am sorry. I never intended to betray anyone, especially you. I love you. I was young, ambitious, desperate. I had all these dreams and plans, and I couldn't get you to listen. I needed to do something worthwhile, needed to become my own man. Can you see that? And selling the land was the only way I saw. I am sorry now."

144

"Hmphh . . ." Will grunted, his eyes fixed firmly on the coffeepot on the table to his left.

"Did you say something, Will?" Arie coaxed.

He glared at her and then turned to Craig.

Kate thought she would fly into a million tiny pieces if Will didn't say something soon. Craig was pale with the same suppressed tension.

Finally the old man spoke. "I never have been much of a listener. Always too busy giving orders. That's what comes of spending your life with cows and sheep."

Craig released his breath in an audible sigh. "Maybe I wasn't a good enough talker, Pop. But I'd like to try now. Okay?"

Will nodded. Then his eyes, brighter than Kate had seen them in weeks, flashed around the room. "Thought you said there was chowder, Arie. Can't you see these young folks are starving! It's been one hell of a morning."

When Will went upstairs for an afternoon nap, Craig and Kate stepped out into the brisk autumn sunlight that drenched the sheltered yard. His arm curved around her waist, and he bent and kissed her gently. His lips were as light and tender as a butterfly's wings, and as quickly gone.

Kate reached up, caught his head between her hands, and drew his face down to her own. She kissed him full on the mouth, letting all her passion center there in that one point of contact. Lips parted, she

145

tasted him. She rasped her tongue across the satin swell of his lower lip, kissed his chin, his throat.

"Whoa, woman, you're making my knees buckle."

"I'd like to do more than that."

He laughed. "Hell, if I had known this was my reward for making peace with my father, I would have swallowed my pride and come back sooner."

Kate bit his earlobe, nuzzled his neck. "It's not a reward; I'm just so happy. Besides, if you had come sooner, I wouldn't have been here."

He caught her to him with such force, it took her breath away. "You know something, Kate? I don't believe that. Somehow—magic, miracle, whatever—you've always been here for me . . . and I've always been here for you!"

"You *are* crazy, Craig Turner!"

"Crazy in love, woman."

Kate tensed and slipped from his arms. Her eyes were dark and shadowed. "Out of the frying pan and into the fire, Turner?"

"I'm already sizzling!"

"I can tell! But we have our own questions to answer, our own problems to work out. Your father wasn't the only obstacle—"

"I can go over, under, around, or through any obstacle you throw in my path, Kate!"

"How about the fact that I work *here,* and you work . . . 'somewhere up north a ways.' Heavens, I don't even know *where* you work, or *what* you do, Mr. Turner."

"Let me show you."

"Now? I have calls this afternoon, and tomorrow."

"Okay, then. Thursday."

"Thursday, my good sir, is Thanksgiving. We'll be having dinner with Will and Arie."

"Friday."

"You are crazy!"

"Then it's a date?"

"I don't know."

"Oh, yes, you do. You just don't want to admit it!"

CHAPTER SEVEN

Thanksgiving arrived amidst frigid temperatures and frosty winds that rushed in off the mountaintops. Lights flickered in the small houses dotting the countryside as families settled down to wide tables groaning beneath the yearly feast. Turkey and sweet potatoes, mounds of mashed potatoes and thick gravy, crusty dressing dotted with oysters and sausage. Pumpkin and mincemeat and pecan pies lined solid wooden sideboards.

The white steeple on the church in the center of Hickory Ridge reached toward the sky and sent peals of ancient chimes upward in a collective thanksgiving. Arie, Will, Kate, and Craig heard the bells and bowed their heads. Each was alone for that moment, gathering their private thoughts and saying their private thanks, before concentrating on Arie's magnificent dinner.

The next day the turkey looked ragged and spent in its corner of the refrigerator. It was Friday.

Craig knocked at the cabin door. "Ready to fly, Kate?"

Kate's hands shook, and she shoved them into the pockets of her wool slacks. She was awash with confusion and desire. Go off with Craig? How reckless! Her heart pounded, but her common sense battled valiantly against the rising demand of her body.

"You can't say no to me, Kate," Craig sliced through her thoughts. "You can't."

And she couldn't.

In less than an hour, Kate and Craig had stopped at the house to say good-bye to Will and Arie, driven to a nearby private airport, and climbed into Craig's plane. They lifted off, the lights of Hickory Ridge dropping away behind them as Craig expertly leveled out his Beechcraft and headed north. Kate felt herself catapulted into a dream, tossed about and rising effortlessly to some untrammeled heights, propelled by a delicious, mysterious force. The fatigue and worry of the past days ebbed from her body and were left behind like the gilded clouds above which they rose and soared. And Kate was filled with a strange euphoria, a peculiar kind of freedom that left her feeling intoxicated, giddy, smiling joyously at the darkening sky beyond the windows. At last she tipped her head and looked directly at Craig.

"Do you have a license?"

Craig laughed, and the deep, mellow timbre of his voice filled her with delight.

"Sir, I happen to be quite serious about this. Consider it a character fault if you will," she teased, "but I *never* fly with unlicensed farmers—"

"Farmer?"

"Well, didn't you say we're going to your farm? Ranch? Oh, Craig! Do you realize I don't even know *where* we're going?"

"Then you can never get lost, beautiful lady." At that moment, the plane dipped slightly and curved to the left. Craig pointed below to where a myriad of soft lights sparkled like diamonds in sunlight. "D.C."

"Oh. Your farm is in D.C.—how clever. Not much competition!"

Again his rich laughter surrounded her, and Kate felt heady with excitement and the nearness of this man, who intrigued her more with every shared moment.

The plane glided gracefully over the nation's capital, and Kate watched the blanket of lights grow thicker and more intense as the plane dipped and curved until at last it rested lightly on a runway at Dulles Airport.

"Almost there, Kate. A forty-five minute drive. And you're going to love it!"

"Love *what*, Craig?"

"Sweetwater Run—the largest and best, if I do say so myself, breeding ranch on the Atlantic coast. We produce what the Kentucky Derby is made of. And

150

it's all hidden away in the thick northern Virginia pines, right in the middle of God's own country."

And hidden away it was, miles along a winding blacktop road that twisted and turned through majestic clusters of pine and hickory and spruce. The full moon, rising now, round and bright, against the blackened sky, beckoned them from a distance. Kate could feel the land rise slowly, almost imperceptibly, as the car, with the ranch's crest emblazoned on its side, made its way up into the hills. At last the thick, clustering forest moved back, and the road widened. Rough-hewn logs bordered the forest's edge leading to a wide gate, which welcomed the world to Sweetwater Run. Small gaslights lit the sign like fireflies dotting the way beyond the entrance. Craig slowed the car and now Kate could see the buildings in the distance, all lit by the same soft gaslights from below and the billowing moon from above.

"Well, darlin', here she is. Welcome to the 'farm.' "

Kate's breath caught in her throat at the sight stretched out before her. She barely heard Craig's voice as he began the deluxe tour. "That big rustic building with the wide porch—that's the main lodge, mess hall for the men, recreation room, and so on. Over there"—he pointed beyond the lodge to a set of cabins built into the side of the woods—"those are the fellas' bunks. And beyond that, which you can't see in the dark, is a field that leads down to the stables. Show you that later." He pulled the car to a halt in front of the lodge and helped Kate out. As she looked around, filling her lungs with the cold, clear air in an attempt to steady her spinning head, she noticed another structure back to the right. It was a large, sprawling two-story house, its natural-wood siding blending into the trees that hugged it on two sides. Large windows looked out onto the land, and along one side an enormous brick chimney climbed up to the sky. "And what is that, Mr. Turner, pray tell?"

"Oh—" Craig looked down at her and grinned. "That, my beautiful guest, is my house. But first, I want you to meet the crew."

Craig guided her quickly up the stone walkway leading to the lodge. She hurried to keep up with his long strides, feeling the excitement flow from his body. She saw the brightness in his eyes as they approached the entrance; why, he was like a young boy showing off his most treasured possessions. And she . . . she was totally overwhelmed. This was not at all what she had expected! But then, she hadn't really known what to expect. Again she felt her head spin and leaned lightly against Craig's side as they moved into the large hall.

A chorus of hellos greeted them from the half dozen men in faded jeans and wool plaid shirts lounging on large overstuffed chairs and couches near a huge stone fireplace. It was echoed from the other end of the room where others were clustered around tables amid a clutter of beer bottles and the plastic click of poker chips.

"Kate!" A familiar voice slid in between the other

friendly hellos. "Kate—hi there! What a wonderful surprise!"

Kate looked around, puzzled for a moment, until her soft green eyes rested on a smiling, bearded face. "Jeremy!" She rushed over to his side and hugged him. "What are you doing up here? Craig didn't tell me! Are you all right?"

Jeremy's eyes flickered in the firelight. "Fit as a fiddle—er . . . a dulcimer." He grinned, planting a friendly kiss on her cheek. "And in answer to your first question, you happen to be looking at the new foreman of Sweetwater Run Ranch!"

Kate's eyes smiled. "Couldn't happen to a nicer guy."

"Hey, McFadden, don't you think we ought to let Kate brighten up some other corner of the room, too!" And with a wink he guided Kate off to meet the other ranch hands.

Kate moved from one group to the next, smiling brightly at the friendly faces and nodding politely. She enjoyed the friendly camaraderie between Craig and the men, and marveled at his diplomacy as he pointed out unique traits of each of the men, areas in which they did particularly well. It was clear that Craig was the boss, but respected and liked rather than feared. There was a feeling of shared achievement in the room that warmed Kate. And the man at her side warmed her, too, until she could feel nothing else but the pressure of his arm upon her arm and the hardness of his chest as he gently brushed against her.

153

Presently they were joined by a short, barrel-chested man, graying slightly at the temples.

"Hi, Ron!" Craig's face broke into a wide smile. "Kate, this is Ron Hilgaard. He's head of the breeding operation here at the ranch. Things have been going so well under his direction that the men have taken to calling him Casanova!"

"That's okay." Ron grinned as he pumped Kate's hand. "I've been called a lot worse!" He turned his broad, weathered face to Kate. "So you're Dr. Harrington, the gorgeous veterinarian responsible for keeping Craig out of our hair these days!"

Kate blushed but felt a surge of pleasure at his words. "Guilty!"

"Well, can't say I blame him a bit!" And he excused himself and went off.

"You know," Craig broke into her thoughts, "Ron meant that about keeping me out of their hair. Things are set up so well at this point they practically run themselves. And Ron has the breeding down so pat I wouldn't dare interfere." There was a note of restlessness in his voice, and Kate let her eyes linger on his face.

"You sound almost sad at your success."

Craig smiled. "No, not exactly. But I did love the ground roots toil and trouble—those struggling beginnings. But you can't stay at ground roots forever. However"—a mysterious sparkle lit his eyes—"you *can* plant the roots somewhere else."

"What? You mean you're thinking of selling all this?"

154

"Oh, no, I'd never do that! I love this place. It's a part of me. But I have been toying with the idea of beginning another ranch further south. Sort of an annex. Move the two-year-olds down where buyers can have easier access to them. Keep this one just for breeding . . . and for an R and R hideaway for me!"

Kate listened carefully, weighing the meaning of the thoughts behind the words. Hoping. But Craig said nothing more, simply led her on to another room. At the far end Kate spotted swinging doors and a hallway leading to a kitchen.

"Ready for some chow, Kate? Bessie always leaves a fridge full of leftovers for midnight snacks."

Kate looked around the cheery room, then up at Craig. "Thanks, but no thanks. For perhaps the first time in my life, I'm too tired to eat."

Craig laughed, low and husky. He reached out and gently squeezed the back of her neck. "What you need, fair lady, is a back rub."

Kate could feel the tensions loosen at the touch of his hand on her neck. She shivered and smiled into his tired face. "Perhaps we *both* need a back rub. Know of any good masseurs?"

"Ah, why it just so happens I do. Come with me." Craig's voice was deep and seductive, and perfectly matched the feeling that was building inside Kate's own body. The two left the lodge and walked up the winding path toward the house nestled in the forest. Craig pulled her close to protect her against the wind. A gust of November air pushed them inside the wide front doors and into the main living room, a

155

two-story area filled with beckoning warmth. The wide fireplace stretching along the north wall was already aglow with leaping flames, their light fused with the soft glow of small lamps. Soft, thick area rugs covered the dark hardwood floor, creating splotches of color that blended enticingly with the comfortable, soft love seats and dark wood tables clustered around the fireplace. A handsome collection of Wyeth prints and paintings of other American artists covered one wall, and on the opposite wall hung a full-sized star pattern quilt in a myriad of earth tones, totally unique in design and color. Craig saw Kate admiring it and said with pride, "My mother made that. Beautiful, isn't it?"

"Oh, yes!" Kate answered, marveling at the lovely things around her. In a handsomely paneled den, filled with brass and polished oak and walnut, he had an incredible display of authentic mountain musical instruments, dating back hundreds of years. In the wide hallway on the second level, she was awed at the loveliest exhibit of equine art—watercolors and prints, sculptures and lithographs—that she had ever seen.

In each room she found herself enjoying the unique and special decorating touches; expensive but always warm, tasteful, and unpretentious. Four large bedroom suites, each with a small sitting room and its own bath, opened off the upstairs hall. "Do you get a lot of company up here?" Kate asked, looking in amazement at the spacious, beautifully appointed suites.

"Oh, now and then. I have an annual horse show in the spring. Buyers come and look over the horses. And friends come up just for the fun of it. The house and all the guest quarters are packed. But most of the time it's pretty empty. The guys all have their own quarters—"

"Well . . . why so big a house, Craig?" Her eyes roamed slowly about the beautiful furnishings, and she thought with silent pleasure how wonderful it would be to spend time in these rooms, enjoying their beauty and peaceful ambience.

"Oh, I don't know. Dreams, I guess. I thought it'd make a fantastic home, or vacation retreat, someday. Room for plenty of kids . . ." His face broke into a grin. "God, how I wish I had had a place like this when I was a kid, a place in which to freely run and roam without barriers or restraints!" Kate watched his expressive face as he explored his dream aloud and was taken by the incongruity of it all—of all these many faces of Craig Turner. How many more dimensions were there to this man? How many more could she handle?

They found themselves back in the firelit living room where Kate immediately dropped onto the thick rug in front of the fire and slipped out of her shoes. She wiggled her toes in the warmth of the fire, oblivious to Craig's careful scrutiny.

There was something about seeing Kate Harrington here in his own home that had struck a chord in Craig Turner. He stood behind the polished wooden bar, pushed in the stereo button, and watched Kate as he filled a tray with two crystal glasses, and a bottle of champagne. The flames flickered on the soft peach of her skin and painted shimmering streaks across her black hair. She tossed her head lightly, and he watched the ebony cascade ripple down her back. He felt an unfamiliar twist in his chest. The desire he understood. That had been there from the day he had watched her talk to that unconscious pig in his father's small operatory. He smiled at the memory. Yes, the desire had been lit immediately. She had a kind of ethereal sensuousness that whipped about him. But he hadn't counted on the strange, nagging, unnerving tugging in his chest. Nor the rush of pure gladness that replaced it when Kate Harrington smiled at him.

Craig Turner had always been a likable loner, with plenty of friends on the fringes when he needed a respite from his solitude. But now he found himself in a peculiar state. He found himself wanting to be with Kate. Wanting to be with her most of the time. No . . . *all* of the time, damn it! And he couldn't figure out why. A most disconcerting state in which to be.

He walked across the thick rugs to her side and handed her a curved, perspiring glass of champagne, deliciously frosted against the intense heat of the fire. Her cheeks were flushed now, painted by the flames' searing heat, and her eyes sparkled in the soft light. Craig slid down beside her.

"Well"—Kate looked up and smiled softly—"shall we toast?"

158

Her eyes were crystal clear, and greener, Craig thought, than the turf on derby day. A deep, verdant hue ringed with gold. "Of course . . . a toast—" But for perhaps the first time in his life, Craig Turner was at a loss for words.

Kate laughed lightly. "Come, then, let me"—she raised her glass, a playful look in her eyes—"to Aunt Arie and her wonderful prescription for tired, bedraggled bodies—"

"Yes." Craig lifted his glass and touched the rim to Kate's, but his thoughts were more intent on the "body" than they were on toasting his kindly aunt. His eyes rested on the sensuous curve beneath Kate's soft sweater, and to Craig's lingering eyes her body looked anything but bedraggled!

The two drank slowly and silently, caught up in the magic of the music and the fire and the waves of fantasy filling the room. Craig had refilled their glasses, and Kate found herself enjoying the delightful headiness that was moving her wonderfully into a magical, carefree world, far away from pressures and decisions and carefully laid out plans.

"Ah, Craig—" She half-closed her eyes and leaned back against the edge of the couch, her shoulders rubbing gently against his own. "Nice . . . this is so nice. I'm beginning to feel like Alice in Wonderland." She looked up at him slowly and touched his lips with the tip of her finger, tracing a fine line around them. "And you, Craig Turner, you're beginning to look a little bit like the Cheshire Cat."

Craig caught her fingers and held them to his lips.

"Guess there's nothing wrong with a little wonderland now and then."

"No." Kate laughed softly. "It certainly can't do any real harm. Unless we get used to it, of course." She felt a touch of sadness and quickly dispelled it with a sip of champagne. The sweet, soothing liquid slid down her throat and melted in with the other warmths: the crackling fire, the shifting moods of Beethoven's *Moonlight Sonata* and—oh, yes—Craig's body, so close and so comfortingly warm. "Say, kind sir"—her thick lashes fluttered teasingly against the flush of her cheeks—"when is that masseur going to arrive? You did promise me one, you know—"

"Ah! The masseur. But, of course." He kissed the tips of her fingers and rose fluidly from the rug. "One moment, please." And he was gone, returning in seconds carrying a large bottle of body oil and a white towel which hung neatly over one arm. He walked sedately over to Kate and bowed solemnly. "Madame, you rang?"

Kate giggled. Her eyes danced as she surveyed the virile, handsome form of the man standing over her. "Dr. Livingstone, I presume?"

"No, no, no!" Craig feigned an injured look. "Your masseur! And the finest, madame, on this entire ranch." Craig knelt down and set his accoutrements on the floor. "I am also discreet, madame. Very discreet. My eyes see nothing but the fine muscles of your lovely back, which need loosening, relaxing. Purely clinical, of course."

"But, of course," Kate murmured as she slipped down upon the thick rug, Craig's bent knees just touching the near side of her body.

Gently, Craig lifted the bottom edge of her sweater, gathered the soft material between his fingers, and slipped it slowly over her head. She heard the rough intake of his breath, the momentary tension in his resumed breathing. Then, with one quick movement, he unsnapped her bra and slipped its narrow straps down her arms. The roughness of the woven rug rubbed against her nipples, bringing them to an excruciating degree of sensitivity, and she felt a deep, aching tremor travel from the tingling tips of her breasts down into her womb, her whole body tightened, pulsing, beginning to throb and to quiver in a transport of passion . . . caught as she was between the soothing warmth of the fire-warmed air and the fierce heat of his flesh so close to hers. Craig hadn't yet touched her, but her whole body was aware of him.

Kate closed her eyes and floated, a whirling, swirling flight. Craig's hands slowly began to caress her shoulders and her neck, firmly, gently, soothingly. The rough pads of his fingertips pressed into her skin; the heel of his palm kneaded her muscles. She could feel his breath on her bare skin as he bent over her, soft breath blown to rekindle the embers to flame . . . and the flames sparked, caught, and burst into a flare of excitement. Her body caught fire beneath his touch. Then unexpectedly, deliciously, the cool oil slid down between her shoulder blades in a tiny river. Craig's palms captured it, smoothing it in rotating circles across her shoulders, back, waist . . . lower and lower until his fingertips slipped ever so lightly beneath the waistband of her slacks. She felt her skin like silk or water beneath his hands, gathered lovingly into his palms, then spread smooth again. Flowing. Fluid. Taking shape and loosing it again beneath his stroking caress. And Kate lost herself and found herself again in his touch. Her curves and lines. The narrowness of her, the round fullness of her, the very definition of her body was dissolved and restored under his hands. There—as she lay still on her pillowed arms—he outlined the winglike span of her shoulder blades, the angle of her bare, gleaming arms, the hard knob of her elbow. Created them. Defined them. There—the balls of his thumbs traced the rolling ridges of her spine, and messages danced there in the cord stretched taut beneath the calloused pads, messages that reached her brain like the sharp retort of fireworks. Flashes of excitement. Flares of lust. And there—he found the round fullness of her breasts, the soft, exaggerated curves of the sides of her breasts, the skin flushed and febrile, waiting, trembling for his touch, her nipples pressed into the weave of the rug as if hiding from the fearsome power of his fingertips. His hands grazed down her unadorned sides, her bare skin yielding in waterlike ripples to his touch. Her nerve endings responded in immediate delight, short-circuiting in ecstasy.

And again his hands edged teasingly beneath her

slacks. "Don't want to get oil on these," Craig said, his voice a husky whisper. And his hands slid beneath her until they found her belt buckle, loosened it, and with one lusty motion tugged off her slacks. Kate moaned, lost in the ecstasy of his touch. She lay upon the rug, the bare expanse of her skin broken only by the mauve lace panties that contrasted softly with her tanned, silky contours.

For a moment Craig rocked back on his heels, taking her with his eyes, swallowing the beauty before him. He could feel himself harden against the tightness of his jeans, could feel his desire swelling, expanding. His breath had quickened, and he basked in the intense emotion that raked his body.

Finally, daring his restraint, he bent once more and resumed the slow, lazy circles down her body, not pausing this time for the thin, restraining panties but slipping them down her long, smooth legs as he pressed the sweetly aromatic oil into her skin.

"Oh, Craig . . ." Kate murmured. "This is heaven!"

"No, my beautiful Kate. We're not nearly there yet. But we'll be there soon. I promise." And his hands continued their spiral journey, pressing against the small of her back, down over her round, firm buttocks, around her thighs and into the graceful curve of her feet. Then back up again . . . all the way to her shoulders.

Languidness soon gave way to the rising ardor that flooded Kate's loins. Craig's touch lingered everywhere, and she felt herself covered completely by his caress, felt the rapturous excitement of his breath upon her skin, his body close to hers. Craig separated his firm fingers and slowly he moved down each side of her body, beneath her arms, until his fingers burrowed beneath her, cupping each waiting breast, full and taut and expectant.

Kate arched her back, peered through the swing of dark hair falling across her cheek, and grinned seductively at her lover. Like a playful kitten, she rolled onto her back and into the curve of his arms, and leaned up to kiss him hard and long on the mouth. "That, kind sir, was quite a massage! Do I leave a tip?"

"A tip, hell!" he growled. "We're heaven-bound, remember? And a ticket will cost you, lady."

"Haven't got a cent on me." She laughed softly, dotting kisses across his mouth. Her fingers twined in his hair.

"That's all right," he breathed against her lips. "I'll take your heart instead." His arms tightened in a crushing hold, and Kate drew him down, down, down on top of her, reveling in the feel of his hard, lusty body.

"Wait, Craig . . . unfair! Here I am naked as a babe, and you've still got your pants on!"

"Lord, woman, ask and you shall receive!" Rocking back on his heels, he crossed his arms over his chest, and in one fluid movement, the muscles knotting and bunching beneath his gleaming skin, he peeled off his sweater and tossed it on the floor. His torso, golden, bare, shone in the firelight. Velvety smooth skin, sleek as an animal's hide. Muscles tensed and defined, catching the firelight's glow on ridge and hollow. Soft brown hair, shades darker than his sun-bleached tawny head, curling across his chest up toward his throat and down across his belly, disappearing into his jeans.

Tipping her body toward him, Kate ran a palm down his front, starting at his throat and trailing her fingers across his chest, circling his nipples, stroking the well-defined muscles of his chest, feeling the invisible tremors shake his body. She trailed her hand down across the curve of his body, down until her palm lay against the top of his jeans. "Need any help?"

Craig swallowed, the sweat beginning to glisten on his forehead and in the dark tangle of hair under his arms.

She leaned over him like a naked sea nymph, a siren . . . and he, the sailor waiting to be drowned, could only nod and whisper "yes" through dry lips.

She pushed him back upon the rug, unzipped the fly of his jeans, and tugged them off. Her hands found and explored every inch of his body.

He moaned and reached for her, wanting to pull her down to him, wanting to love her . . . but she resisted, shaking her dark head, her eyes sparkling.

"Oh, no. Not yet. This is tit for tat. It's only fair . . ." And she continued to stroke him, murmuring sweetly as her hands coaxed him to passion's edge. "You're beautiful—as beautiful as any statue in a museum You're Adonis and Apollo . . . you're—"

"You're making me wild, woman!" His mouth smothered hers, and he kissed her deeply, draining her of energy and will. He rolled onto his side and pulled her to him, snuggling his lusty length to her soft womanhood and resting his hand on her damp flank. They kissed again, whispered and coaxed and teased against each other's mouths, lips, and tongues, animated with impatient, precarious joy. Mouths trailed across flesh, tasting every surface of the other's unresisting body. Legs entwined, hips thrust together, they wriggled and writhed, buffeted by shivers of delight, yearning and straining to become one, to get past the boundaries of skin and bone and muscle . . . to become one.

His passion riding him like a harsh master, Craig slid his hands beneath her hips, lifting Kate to him, wild with love and need.

And Kate felt herself riding a tide of ecstasy as he filled her, his strength and beauty bursting within her, pervading every fiber, every crevice.

And he, the sailor swept upon the rocks, drowning in delight, a smile upon his still face.

And she, mermaid wrapped in dark tangles of hair, riding the waves of her satisfaction, lay satiated, subdued in his arms.

"Is this heaven, Craig?"

"Got to be, Kate. Sure is somewhere I've never been before."

CHAPTER EIGHT

Outside the wide bedroom window the earth was dusted with its first, soft covering of snow. The morning sun struck the crystal sheen and exploded into welcoming rays of daylight. The slim line of the horizon stretched across the hills in a red streak as the sun slowly edged itself into the sky. Above the pines there was still blackness, slowly moving into light as a new day began.

Craig, dressed in faded jeans and a heavy wool shirt, stood at the window watching nature's drama as it prepared for another act. Then he turned and walked slowly back to the large four-poster bed. Centered against the soft sheets and down comforter, Kate slept, her slender body curled like a furled rosebud. Craig bent over the enticing form and kissed

Kate lightly on the tip of her ear. "Good morning, my love," he whispered into her sleep.

Kate stirred and a smile spread automatically across her lips. Slowly her eyelids fluttered and she met his gaze, bringing herself to wakefulness. "Craig . . ." Her voice was soft and sleep-coated. "Good morning, Craig." Kate felt the luxuriousness of their passion still coating her, the balmy wash of after-love bathing her in its sweet breath. She closed her eyes and burrowed deeper beneath the quilt.

"Oh, no, you don't, Kate." Craig's voice was strong now and full of morning life. "It's morning, lovely lady, time to rise and shine—" And with a swoop he swept the coverings from the bed.

Kate's naked body shivered in the cool breeze, trembling like a fragile branch as every nerve responded to the onslaught of air. "Craig!" she screeched, and reached futilely for the covers.

His hearty laugh filled the room, and he reached for her smooth, supple body, grabbing her firmly around the wrist. "Come on, Kate—stop acting like a city girl! It's way past dawn . . . almost five thirty already!"

Kate's groan bounced off the walls and echoed with such intensity that both she and Craig were suddenly shaking with laughter. "Darn you," Kate managed between chuckles. And with her one free hand she reached behind her until her fingers sunk firmly into a pillow. With a swish and a holler she planted it directly on Craig's head, then slipped from beneath his grasp, skittering naked across the room.

Craig countered with a mighty thrust of the remaining pillow. It nicked Kate's chin, barreled against the wall, and exploded in a flurry of feathery rain. In an instant he was at her side, his arms about her narrow waist, lifting her high into the air. "Aha! There's wild filly in you, Kate Harrington! I should have guessed." And he deposited her flat in the middle of the bed, pinning her down with the weight of his chest. His fingers sent delicious shivers of delight spearing through her body.

"My, my," Kate choked. "This is a most interesting position in which to find oneself!"

Craig shifted and let his body fall down beside hers. "Dear Dr. Harrington, you'd better vanish immediately and come back with something on your frame other than that beautiful curve of silky skin. Or we will never leave this room today!"

Kate eyed him with a sudden air of coquettishness. "Oh? And you object, kind sir?" But before he could answer, she slipped from the bed and into the adjoining dressing room, leaving a *very* uncomfortable Craig fidgeting on the bed.

The two jacketed figures walked across the frozen crunch of grass toward the stables, their bodies casting eerie shadows upon the white sheet beneath them. Above, the moon and the sun cavorted together in the dawning sky, vying for position. Craig held Kate's mittened hand tightly in his own, and the two walked briskly against the sharp wind. Slung over Craig's free arm was a large wicker basket, filled with breakfast, he told Kate.

"Ah, stable staples." She laughed and squeezed the possessive fingers holding her own. She moved closer, linking her body to his. Kate was basking in their wonderland, knowing somewhere, way back in the shadows of her mind, that it would soon end. But she would not allow such faraway knowledge to tarnish the moment, the dream. No, this was her moment and she wasn't going to give it up, not for security . . . safety . . . Not for today, at least.

They passed by neat rows of fences and carefully leveled circular tracks. The flattened area and wide fields were surrounded by dense woods, a hollowed-out haven for the horses. Several stables stretched back, one after another, until they touched the edge of the woods. Craig held her hand as they stepped into the first building. The whinnying of the ponies greeted them in the early morning light. Soft, damp hay rustled beneath their feet, and the air was thick with a moist, horsey smell.

He caught her in a warm, impulsive hug. "Come, let me introduce you to my friends." At each stall they paused, and above each half-door the finely boned, beautifully curved head of a thoroughbred horse would appear. Bay and roan, gray and chestnut . . . wide gentle eyes, tapering faces, snuffling velvety noses. They nudged and pushed at Craig's familiar shoulder and for each he reached into the basket and withdrew a slice of apple, a chunk of carrot . . . and for each a fond caress and gentle word.

170

"Craig, they're so beautiful . . ."

"Glad you like my family. I can see they like you, too." He laughed as a roan mare gently nuzzled Kate's neck.

"Here, Candelight, let's let you out for a while. There's plenty of hay in the back pasture."

The horse followed them out of the barn with light, quick steps. It blew its breath on Craig's collar, accepted a last piece of carrot, and trotted on.

Craig led Kate on to the building farthest away.

"This is going to be the new foaling stable," he explained. "We just finished it; put the roof on last Friday." He ran his hand down the smooth, planed board, tracing the knots and whorls in the wood's grained surface. "Pretty, isn't it?"

"As stables go . . ." Kate teased.

"Hey! This here's my pride and joy. I expect a little enthusiasm!"

"All my enthusiasm is reserved for other things right now."

"Such as?" he asked, hugging her close.

"Such as a warm place, out of this wind."

"Uhh uhh. Try again." He grinned, slipping his hand inside her jacket.

"Breakfast?"

"Wrong again!"

"This?" She rose onto tiptoe and kissed his lips, a long, lingeringly sweet kiss. "Enough enthusiasm?" Giggling, she watched his eyes shine.

Together they stepped into the stable. Early sunlight streamed like angel's breath down upon the

171

golden hay. The air was filled with the scent of mown grass and clover and the sweet hint of alfalfa. The rafters seemed a hundred miles above them, and dust motes danced like fairies in the still, silent air.

"Looks like some fairy-tale princess was in here spinning all night, doesn't it, Craig?" Kate whispered into the vaulted hush.

"You're the only princess I ever want to see here—and this is enough of a fairy tale for me."

Craig stepped to the first stall, pulled a blanket from a nearby rack, spread it on the ground, and patted the space beside him. "Breakfast is served."

Kate sat down, knees drawn up, chin resting on the back of one hand. She watched Craig open the basket, pour two glasses of champagne, and lift out a tiny crate of perfect, plump red strawberries.

"Mmm, this must be a fairy tale or a dream"—she smiled, accepting the proffered glass—"and you are the knight on the white horse." She lifted her glass. "To dreams." Her heart filled with the wish that her life were but a succession of such dreams.

Craig seemed caught by the same bittersweet wistfulness. A smile of great tenderness and hopefulness lit his face. A small pulse beat at his temple. His eyes darkened to the color of slate, intense and searching. "Are you happy, Kate? I am . . . very happy." A shy, soft laugh rumbled in his throat. "Remember that old song?

"Today, while the blossoms still cling to the vine,
I'll taste your strawberries and drink your sweet
    wine.

172

A million tomorrows will all pass away,
Ere I forget all the joys that are mine today."

His voice was a rich, mellow baritone, untrained but lovely to the ear. And the song—his singing of it here, to her alone—brought tears to Kate's eyes. She turned away and lifted her glass to trembling lips, embarrassed by the rush of emotion that had filled her . . . and its depth.

But he knelt beside her, lifted the glass from her hand, and placed his mouth where the glass had been, there on her sweet lips.

"Oh, Kate, never, never . . . have I felt this way."

She rubbed her cheek against the roughness of his shaven face. "Nor I, Craig."

Their lovemaking was sweet and slow, and never would she forget how the stillness seemed to accept and welcome their love-filled cries of passion.

Afterward, they lay on the straw, naked, robed in each other's arms. Kate was sipping her champagne when something wet and cold nipped along her thigh.

"Oh!" she gasped, startled, then laughed. They both turned to see a sleek brown head nudging her again, its rough tongue happily licking the salt from her bare skin. "Candlelight seems to have joined us. I think she's trying to tell me something!"

They both laughed and dressed and sat munching strawberries in the straw, oblivious for that special moment, that any other world existed outside of that small, body-heated stall at Sweetwater Run Ranch.

"Craig? Craig—you in here?" Ron Hilgaard's voice boomed through the sun-streaked interior of the barn. "Craig?"

Craig leapt to his feet and brushed the hay from his hastily smoothed pants and shirt. "In here, Ron. Be with you in a minute." He threw Kate a silent kiss, and she answered with a seductive smile.

"Morning, Ron. What's up?" He greeted the breeding foreman with polished calm, broken only by an undisciplined smile playing at the corners of his mouth.

"Seems you got a phone call from Hickory Ridge— actually the woman asked to speak to either you or Kate Harrington. Bessie took the message and seemed to think one of you should return right away. You know I would never have tracked you down like this if it didn't sound important." He winked teasingly at Craig.

"No problem—thanks for tracking me down," Craig answered, and headed back to the stall.

"I heard . . ." Kate said as he turned into the stall. She was brushing her jeans free of the dry straw that stubbornly clung to them, and quickly buttoned her blouse. "Craig, what do you suppose is wrong? Arie wouldn't call here unless—"

"Unless what, Kate? You have no idea that there is anything wrong at all, so don't start jumping to conclusions. Arie's getting on in years, forgetful. She may have just misplaced the vitamin supplement for Mrs. Garvey's Siamese."

174

Kate forced a laugh as she pulled on her jacket. "Arie? Misplace something? Never! But you're probably right, I shouldn't borrow trouble. But I would like to hurry back to call, Craig—if you don't mind."

He drew his fingers along the curve of her face and savored the look of pleasure still lingering there. "I mind like hell . . . but come on, let's go."

The two quickly collected the breakfast debris, slipped everything back into the basket, and headed toward the house.

"Kate . . ." Craig broke the silence as they walked quickly along the path. "Kate, I've got to talk to you. Now, before Will and Arie and all of that jump back into our lives. Kate . . ."

Kate's eyes widened as she waited for him to continue.

"Kate, do you like it here?"

"Of course I do, Craig. It's beautiful."

"Could you be happy here?"

"What?" The smile slowly slipped from her eyes, though it lingered like a habit on her lips. "What do you mean?"

"Kate. I love you. I knew it this morning while I was watching you sleep. Well, I've known it for a while, I guess. I want to marry you." His voice was intimate and warm and vibrating with emotion. "Kate, I had felt it all this time and never given it a name, never said the words aloud. But I love you. And I can't live without you. Can't. Won't."

Kate slipped into the warm circle of his arms and leaned her cheek against the warm, steady pulse at his throat. "I love you, too, Craig Turner." She turned and let her lips touch his flesh. "I love you, too."

His arms tightened their hold. "Then what do you say? Could you be happy here? You could be Sweetwater Run's own private vet? I could build you a clinic . . . and . . ."

"No, Craig." She pressed two fingers to his lips and held them there. "Craig, I love you. But I love my work. And Hickory Ridge and the animals that roam those hills. Your father and Arie and all those people who trust me, who need me, especially now with Will . . . I love the welcome in their eyes, the confidence. Oh, Craig"—she pulled his face down to hers and kissed him, held him—"I don't love any of those things, not any one of them, as much as I love you. But they are the life I've made. I . . . I don't think I could go on without them."

"Kate, my Kate, I'll build you a new life."

"Craig. This is the life *I've* built. It's part of me. No, it *is* me. Who I am. The woman you love." She shook her head, tears standing in her eyes, but her chin was firm. "I think we both need to think about this."

"Think? I can't think of life without you. I couldn't wake up in the morning knowing you were walking, moving, smiling—somewhere else! Kate, I—"

"Wait," she whispered, holding him close. They were standing near the house now. "Wait, dear heart. Let me call, and then we'll talk."

Craig followed her up the steps, slipped off his jacket, and walked over to the unlit fireplace. His head was filled with a loud buzzing, and a sharp pain

176

gnawed somewhere in his chest. She had to love him! She said she did, but she hadn't said she would stay. It wasn't possible. How could she love him as much as he loved her and even *think* of being away from him? He wiped away the sweat that had sprung to his brow and stared into the fireplace. How could she choose anything over him? *He* knew he couldn't live without her! His heart stopped. His eyes cleared. The pain vanished. No, he couldn't. Wouldn't. His heart began to beat again, loud and steady and sure.

Then Kate stepped back into the room. The freshness and glow had faded from her lovely face.

"It's Will . . ." Her voice was small and thin. "He's had a stroke. We need to go home."

The plane soared above the clouds, swallowing up the miles between Sweetwater Run and Hickory Ridge. Both Craig and Kate were silent, each absorbed in their own thoughts. Arie had assured Kate it was a small stroke and that only his speech seemed to have been affected. He was in good hands, she had insisted, at the county hospital. But Kate's feeling of guilt and sadness washed away any reassurance of his well-being. She had left Will . . . left him alone at the clinic. Slowly she felt herself filling to the brim with tears; they rolled slowly down her cheeks.

Craig leaned over and wiped them away. "Kate, it'll be all right. Don't worry. Arie said it'll be all right, and we'll be there soon."

CHAPTER NINE

Three days later Kate sat on the hard, unforgiving surface of a chair in the hospital cafeteria. She ached with tiredness, stiff muscles, tension. Her coffee was cold. Her sandwich lay uneaten before her.

The doctor had assured Kate and Craig that Will was going to be fine and would leave the hospital in just a few days with only a few minor restrictions. "We'll just have to tune him down a bit, Kate. Get him moving at a slower pace. But don't you worry yourself. Doc Turner is made of indestructible stuff," the physician had said, laughing.

But Kate was still filled with worry and concern. These hills without Will Turner? These hills *were* Will Turner. He'd touched every inch of them and every person living on the deep, rich soil. Most of all he had touched her. And for that reason alone Kate owed him so much. And loved him. But still her heart ached with another love.

A movement at the cafeteria's entrance side-tracked her thoughts, and she looked up into Arie's kindly face.

"Here you are, Kate. Craig sent me to find you. He's got Will dressed and ready to go." Arie's fond gaze swept over Kate, and she smiled. "It will be all right, dear. You'll see."

Kate's heels tap-tapped along the pale green tile floors, Arie's rubber-soled shoes a soft echo at her side.

"Come child, hurry. They're going to have to tie that old coot down if we don't get him out of here this instant! Hurry."

Laughing, the older woman rapped lightly on the door to Will's room. His old, battered suitcase sat propped by the doorway. His coat lay tossed across his bed. And Will himself stood by the window, hat on, scarf already wound around his neck.

"Well, hallelujah! Here you are, girl. Thought you decided to run away for Christmas—holidays seem to have that effect on you!"

"No chance, Will Turner. I'm here to take your ornery self back to the clinic where you belong."

"Sure. I know your type. You just don't want to handle all the work there is to be done all by yourself. What's the problem? Mrs. Garvey's puss need a second alteration?"

"Hush, you two," Arie scolded, pushing his coat at

the old vet. "They'll throw us out of here if you both carry on this way."

"That's the idea! Right, Katie, my girl?"

"Right, Doc!"

Arie looked like a flustered mother hen, shooing her two unruly chicks down the empty, sterile hospital halls. The three spilled happily, noisily out into the winter sunshine.

In moments they were parked in front of the clinic. Craig helped Will and Arie from the Land Rover and held the door open to let them both on into the clinic's familiar warmth. Kate almost fell over Will when he stopped short in the doorway.

"What? What's happened?"

Looking past them, Kate noticed a most surprising thing: The rear wall of the building was gone. In its place was a thick sheet of plastic, which succeeded in keeping the wind out although the room's temperature had fallen drastically. "What—what's going on?"

Tugging on a spattered painting cap over his sandy hair, his sky-blue eyes dancing with mischief, Craig wore the widest grin since the Cheshire Cat. "So, what do you think?"

"Are you crazy, boy? What have you done to my clinic?"

"Oh, Craig—you *are* crazy!" Kate sidestepped the obstacles in her path and hurried to his side. Fists balled at her sides, her chin jutting furiously up at him, her eyes sparking fire, she hissed, "What *is* going on? Your father—the poor man just had a stroke and you'll give him another! And our clinic . . . our beautiful clinic . . ."

"Oh, Kate . . . my beautiful Kate," Craig said, laughing, wrapping her in a bear hug that left her weak and trembling. "This is the site of your new laboratory. State of the art, up to the minute. A brand-new lab. No more waiting days, weeks, for lab reports, for Coggins results. Nope! You're both too good for that. It is my present to you. Here are the plans and blueprints."

"A present," Will repeated hoarsely, looking carefully at the unrolled stack of designs. His old fingers trailed lovingly over the proposed area: the counters and work stations, the professionally designed space, the efficient equipment, the time- and step-saving layout. "A present . . ."

"Yes, a present! From me to you. And look, Pop, it will have a great, huge bay window back here, so you can look out over these hills and fields you love so much."

Kate let her cheek brush lightly against Craig's broad shoulder. "You *are* crazy, Craig Turner. And the nicest man I've ever met."

Craig nuzzled her cheek and whispered, "I'll let you tell me that again, as soon as we get the old folks settled, and we slip away. . . ."

She hugged the breath right out of his lanky frame. "That's a deal!"

181

CHAPTER TEN

They slipped away in no time. Will and Arie chased them off, claiming all the excitement had worn them out. It might have been true, but Kate thought she saw sparkles in their eyes.

Kate, however, did not feel like sparkling. As ever, she welcomed the weight of Craig's arm about her shoulders, savored the nearness of his body, delighted in the warmth of his smile.

But now they would have to continue that long-delayed talk begun at Sweetwater Run. The problems were still there, a constant ache in her heart. Still Kate had no solutions.

"Okay, woman, tell me again how I'm the best thing you've ever seen!" Craig said with playful insistence as they stepped out onto the sidewalk in front of the clinic.

"Don't go twisting my words now, mister," she teased, brushing the hair back from his eyes with one gloved hand. "What I said was you're the nicest man I ever met."

"All right, I'll settle for a repeat of that!"

She spoke the words softly, with love.

"Hey, why are you looking so sad, darlin'? Everything's going to be just fine."

Without knowing she was going to, Kate turned and flung herself into his arms. Right there, in the middle of Main Street again, just when Hickory Ridge had just about given up hope.

"Oh, Craig, I can't stand it anymore. I can barely stand to wake up in the mornings. I open my eyes and see my room, hear the sounds outside my window, smell the pines I've walked through and dreamed in. But it's no good. It wouldn't be good without *you*. But I just don't know . . . don't know how . . ."

"Hush, darlin'." He kissed her wet face, holding her as gently as a newborn foal. "Hush. It's going to be all right. I promise. Trust me?"

"With all my heart."

"Then let's go back to the cabin. You look ready to fall over. Let's go back to where it's quiet, and private"—he winked—"and we'll . . . talk!"

First Kate soaked in a steamy, bubble-filled tub, scented with the delicate lemon salts Craig found irresistible. Then she brushed her ink-dark hair until it fell in soft waves about her face and down over her shoulders. Her skin was pale and clear, lit from within by a gentle glow of happiness. There were dapples of cameo-pink color high on her cheekbones. Her green eyes, ringed with dark lashes, shone with the joy that only love can bring.

She didn't hurry. Craig was waiting out there, just a room away, but suddenly Kate felt as if she had all the time in the world. He had said to trust him, and she did. Completely. Somehow their lives would mesh, become one. Because they had to. And because Craig had asked her to trust him, and she had seen the love light burning in his eyes.

So she didn't hurry, at least not too much, and she smiled at her reflection in the glass. "Yes, it was right. Better than right—perfect."

She slipped into a soft robe, knotted the belt loosely about her waist, and opened the door.

Craig lay in bed, his torso bare above the cover's edge. The outer muscles of his chest strained and slid as he breathed, trying to control his excitement. His jaw was tight with tension.

"Been waiting long?" Kate murmured.

"Come here, babe, come here," he said, tossing back the cover.

Kate stretched out alongside him, and Craig rolled onto one side and wrapped her in his embrace. "Feeling better?"

"Yes." She laughed softly. "Though I don't know why."

"Let me tell you why. You see, there was this fella. Fell head over heels in love with this gal. Problem was, they lived, and worked, hundreds of miles apart."

"Poor things," Kate purred. "How terrible for them."

"Nope. No problem at all. Cause this fella, he realized that this gal he loved had to live where she did. Her job and all kinds of special feelings were wrapped up in the place. But the fella—Hell, he could raise horses anywhere!"

"Oh, Craig!" Kate gasped, the tears leaping to her eyes. "Oh, dearest, I couldn't ask you to do that!"

"You don't have to ask. It's already done. Pop sold me a piece of land, and next spring, when you look out that clinic window, you'll see our horses grazing on the slopes. And one day, maybe you'll be watching a child or two out that same window—"

Kate looked at his beloved face. His grin gently turned into a loving smile, and he leaned over her and showered her with a multitude of adoring kisses. "Think you can face getting up in the mornings now?"

"I think I'll be looking forward to mornings—and nights—from now on. And I've got a good idea about how to fill some of those hours in between."

"Really?"

"Really. Want to join me?" Her fingers unfastened the knot at her waist, and she let the robe fall open.

Craig let first his eyes, and then his hands, travel the smooth, silken length of her body.

Kate embarked on her own delicious journey of exploration.

And when they made love, it was like coming home.

LOOK FOR NEXT MONTH'S
CANDLELIGHT ECSTASY ROMANCES®

Candlelight Ecstasy Romances™

$1.95 each

At your local bookstore or use this handy coupon for ordering:

DELL BOOKS
P.O. BOX 1000, PINE BROOK, N.J. 07058-1000   B215A

Please send me the books I have checked above. I am enclosing $ _____ (please add 75c per copy to cover postage and handling). Send check or money order—no cash or C.O.D.'s. Please allow up to 8 weeks for shipment.

Name _____

Address _____

City _____ State Zip _____

Candlelight Ecstasy Romances™

$1.95 each

All-new
Candlelight Newsletter

An exceptional, *free* offer awaits readers of Dell's incomparable Candlelight Ecstasy and Supreme Romances.

Subscribe to our all-new CANDLELIGHT NEWSLETTER and you will receive—at absolutely no cost to you—exciting, exclusive information about today's finest romance novels and novelists. You'll be part of a select group to receive sneak previews of upcoming Candlelight Romances, well in advance of publication.

You'll also go behind the scenes to "meet" our Ecstasy and Supreme authors, learning firsthand where they get their ideas and how they made it to the top. News of author appearances and events will be detailed, as well. And contributions from the Candlelight editor will give you the inside scoop on how she makes her decisions about what to publish—and how *you* can try your hand at writing an Ecstasy or Supreme.

You'll find all this and more in Dell's CANDLELIGHT NEWSLETTER. And best of all, *it costs you nothing.* That's right! It's Dell's way of thanking our loyal Candlelight readers and of adding another dimension to your reading enjoyment.

Just fill out the coupon below, return it to us, and look forward to receiving the first of many CANDLELIGHT NEWSLETTERS—overflowing with the kind of excitement that only enhances our romances!

Return to: DELL PUBLISHING CO., INC.   B215E
        Candlelight Newsletter • Publicity Department
        245 East 47 Street • New York, N.Y. 10017

Name_____

Address_____

City_____

State_____ Zip_____

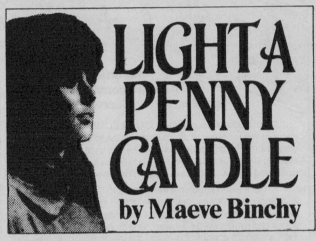